PATCHWORK

ALSO IN THE NVLA SERIES

The Plotinus

RIKKI DUCORNET

We're Safe When We're Alone

NGHIEM TRAN

Cecilia

K-MING CHANG

Sound Museum

POUPEH MISSAGHI

PATCHWORK

Tom Comitta

COFFEE HOUSE PRESS
Minneapolis
2025

Copyright © 2025 by Tom Comitta
Cover design by Sarah Evenson
NVLA series design by Rachel Holscher
Author photo © Beowulf Sheehan

Coffee House Press books are available to the trade through our primary distributor, Consortium Book Sales & Distribution, cbsd.com or (800) 283-3572. For personal orders, catalogs, or other information, write to info@coffeehousepress.org.

All rights reserved.

Coffee House Press is a nonprofit literary publishing house. Support from private foundations, corporate giving programs, government programs, and generous individuals helps make the publication of our books possible. We gratefully acknowledge their support in detail in the back of this book.

LIBRARY OF CONGRESS CATALOGING-IN-PUBLICATION DATA

Names: Comitta, Tom, 1985– author.
Title: Patchwork / Tom Comitta.
Description: Minneapolis : Coffee House Press, 2025.
Identifiers: LCCN 2024057054 (print) | LCCN 2024057055 (ebook) | ISBN 9781566897297 (paperback) | ISBN 9781566897303 (epub)
Subjects: LCGFT: Novellas.
Classification: LCC PS3603.O4776 P38 2025 (print) | LCC PS3603.O4776 (ebook) | DDC 813/.6—dc23/eng/20241216
LC record available at https://lccn.loc.gov/2024057054
LC ebook record available at https://lccn.loc.gov/2024057055

PRINTED IN THE UNITED STATES OF AMERICA

32 31 30 29 28 27 26 25 1 2 3 4 5 6 7 8

The NVLA series is an artistic playground where authors challenge and broaden the outer edges of storytelling. Each novella illuminates the capacious and often overlooked space of possibilities between short stories and novels. Unified by Sarah Evenson's bold and expressive series design, NVLA places works as compact as they are complex in conversation to demonstrate the infinite potential of the form.

For my friend and editor, Lizzie Davis

PATCHWORK

We are all patchwork, and so shapeless and diverse
in composition that each bit, each moment, plays its own game.

—*Montaigne*

I

BEING THE FIRST LINES OF THIS NOVEL

AND 65 OTHER NOVELS

Dear Anyone Who Finds This,

If you're going to read this, don't bother. If you are interested in stories with happy endings, you would be better off reading some other book. I am a sick man . . . I am a spiteful man. I have never begun a novel with more misgiving.

If you really want to hear about it, the first thing you'll probably want to know is where I was born, and what my lousy childhood was like, and how my parents were occupied and all before they had me, and all that David Copperfield kind of crap, but I don't feel like going into it, if you want to know the truth. If I speak of myself in this story, it is because I have been deeply involved in its startling events. Whether I shall turn out to be the hero of my own life, or whether that station will be held by anybody else, these pages must show.

I, Tiberius Claudius Drusus Nero Germanicus This-that-and-the-other (for I shall not trouble you yet with all my titles), was once, and not so long ago either, known to my friends and relatives and associates as "Claudius the Idiot," or "That Claudius," or "Claudius the Stammerer," or "Clau-Clau-Claudius," or at best as "Poor Uncle Claudius." I was born in 1927, the child of middle-class parents, both English, and themselves born in the grotesquely elongated shadow, which they never rose sufficiently above history to leave, of that monstrous dwarf Queen Victoria. Like most people I lived for a long time with my mother and father. My father had a face that could stop a clock. My Mother, whose Relations were named Robinson, she was coughing, always coughing, and sometimes she coughed up blood.

My father had a small estate in Nottinghamshire: I was the third of five sons. We were the Mulvaneys, remember us? On my naming day when I come 12, I gone front spear and kilt a wyld boar. When he was nearly thirteen, my brother Jem got his arm broken badly at the elbow. On an exceptionally hot evening in 1938, the Rutherford girl had been missing for eight days when my brother John returned home and found a monster waiting in his house. The entire affair is shrouded in mystery . . .

But I digress. When I first found employment with Lance Lovelace, I had not yet attained my majority, while he was over sixty. August the First, 19—, I took my degree of Doctor of Medicine of the University of London, and Christmas Eve, 1955, I first saw the light in the city of Boston.

The first time I saw Catherine she was wearing a vivid crimson dress and was nervously leafing through a magazine in my waiting room. It was late in the spring. Her hair was a brilliant green. It was love at first sight.

In the late summer of that year we lived in a house in a village that looked across the river and the plain to the mountains. The town lay sprawled over half a square mile, always so lively, so neat, and so trim that one might believe every day to be Sunday, with its shady park, with its tall trees, spreading over its riverrun, past Eve and Adam's. It was a soft, reposeful summer landscape, as lovely as a dream.

It was like so, but wasn't. I do not quite know how it happened, my recollection of the whole matter ebbing in a somewhat clouded condition, but by the usual Corruption of Words, I will tell you: one afternoon, in the shade of the house, in the sunshine of the riverbank near the boats, we wanted more. I had been busy all day trying to swarm the bees and secure my honey. She had been reclining, seething and angry. The sun shone, having no alternative, on the nothing new.

It was a wrong number that started it, the telephone ringing three times in the dead of night. The voice of the clergyman? Manfred, Prince of Otranto? Monte Irvin, alderman of the city and prospective Lord Mayor of London? I was not sure. Like a match struck in a darkened room, like the brief doomed flare of exploding suns that registers dimly on blind men's eyes, the beginning of the horror passed almost unnoticed. But my dear angel was looking out of the window with many expressions of interest . . .

Not long after my wife and I split up, my suffering left me sad and gloomy; I began to discover I was not the person I wanted to be. I was already past my prime. I was genuinely tired. I was the shadow of the waxwing slain by the false azure in the windowpane. I was one hundred miles from Nowhere.

For a long time, I went to bed early. I would lie in bed and watch the show, how bees squeezed through the cracks of my bedroom wall and flew circles around the room, making that propeller sound, a high-pitched *zzzzzz* that hummed along my skin. "I wonder when in the world you're going to do anything?" said my brother's wife.

The letter that would change everything arrived on a Tuesday. "Here's a letter for you, Doctor," said the housekeeper, as she entered the plain room used as a library and sitting-room. I choked and cursed and spat and threw the paper to the floor. Having placed in my mouth sufficient bread for three minutes' chewing, I withdrew my powers of sensual perception and retired into the privacy of my mind, my eyes and face assuming a vacant and preoccupied expression. After a while, everything started to blur. My brain was drowning in grease.

I dare say that I had already read my uncle's letter a hundred times, and I am sure that I knew it by heart. In offering the following pages to the public, I should like it to be known that no interviewer has extracted them from me by the thumbscrew of a morning call, nor have they been wheedled out of me by the caresses of those iron-maidens of literature, the publishers.

II

BEING THE CONTENTS OF MY UNCLE'S LETTER

My Nephew, the Signorino,

You were expecting me to call? Didn't you receive our letter? In the letter it's all explained, we sent it some time ago, the mail is so slow these days, you'll receive it of course. Anyway, none of that can help you now! Here you are again. All messed up and no place to go. I'm crying because of how sad you are. You have little cause to rejoice. You are hurt. You sulk because you can't stop thinking of her.

What you need is a good pep talk from Ted Allagash, but he is not to be found. What you need is some lunch to set you right. As I'm sure you know, a good, long session of weeping can often make you feel better, even if your circumstances have not changed one bit.

I'll wager you and I have something in common. "Oh, I doubt that," you say, I'm sure. There's time to convince you otherwise: You (and I, too) come from the country. You were convinced of the importance of your job and the inevitability of rising above it. You met people you had admired half your life. You got married. You were gathering experience for a novel. I, too, would like to erase myself and find another I, another voice, another name, to be reborn in a book, a truth not contaminated by the dominant pseudo truths. The thing is, although we are both former students of the same instructor, my age is quite advanced. Time is something I cannot control. You have many years of earning ahead of you. You have a whole life ahead.

You might say that it is hardly worth while to labour the point, yes, but I need you to run an errand for me. It's first and foremost a matter of security and second because there is always something essential that remains outside the written sentence (you need to relax and get on with business—you have a mortgage yourself, do you not?).

This is the story: I am acquainted with a nobleman, who has lost a handsome snuff box—beautiful repoussé work, with his arms engraved on the lid. Now that it is stolen, it must be recovered without delay. "That's my job," you say, yes? Da? I hopo so. You ask yourself, "His snuff box? You don't mean to say that they are making all this fuss over a trifling thing like a snuff box?" Of course, there must have been something inside the box, else why should any one have stolen it?

I know that you have many questions, and all will be answered fully. For what I've told you is only the beginning . . . because you yourself are debating departing, yes? You see yourself as the kind of guy who appreciates a quiet night at home with a good book. A little Mozart on the speakers, a cup of cocoa on the arm of the chair, slippers on the feet. But now, now there is a different person. You are an unwilling emissary from the land of pedantry, and now a wild chase after a snuff box calls for you.

Congratulations! This is the best news you've heard since the last time the Fed lowered interest rates. Your apartment is a chamber of horrors. There are instruments of torture in the kitchen cabinets, rings in the walls, spikes on the bed. That place is must-to-avoid. Now you have got your land legs back to carry out a mission without too much difficulty.

When you get up to leave, take deep breaths. Get dressed. Elect not to drive your car. (You still owe thirty grand on that Porsche, and with your current streak of luck, you definitely could count on bashing it against something inflexible.) Leave immediately. Walk through wooded areas, cross the ocean, explore the continent beneath the Southern Cross – a landscape that only you can see and desire – until you can find the latest hiding place of the snuff box!

Well, what are you waiting for? Aren't you tired of reading? Stretch your legs. Think of Socrates, the kind of guy who accepted his cup and drank it down. Cling to the hope that you will somehow escape your fate. Meanwhile, would you please tell your brother John I called? . . . But anyway, it doesn't matter, I'll call back. Thanks a lot.

–Uncle Hibal

III

BEING MY RESPONSE TO THE LETTER

"Nay, sir," I could not avoid answering aloud.

No.

I'd rather not!

I thowt I *could* do
that! But nah.

I will not be coerced! Oh no! And neither will John! There is more going on than meets the eye . . .

I cannot bear it—I cannot!

Never!

Ay—nay.

Nay, you'll not drive me off again. You were really sorry for me, were you? Well, there was cause. I've fought through a bitter life since, nay, Cathy.

Nay, there's no comprehending it.

Nay, you'll be ashamed of me every day of your life.

Nay! it fair brusts my heart!

No way, dude.

Then about two days after this snub, I was coming down the stairs of the main house when I found Moira B. just behind me. Her bright blue eyes went round.*

---

* How blue? Bluer far and of a different quality than the Nature metaphors which were both engine and fuel to so much of precedent literature. A fine, modern, acid, synthetic blue; the shiny cerulean of the skies on postcards sent from lush subtropics; the promising, fat, unnatural blue of the heavy tranquillizer capsule; the cool, mean blue of that fake kitchen sponge; the deepest, most unbelievable azure of the tiled and mossless interiors of California swimming pools—it might have dispirited the observer had it not glittered like a chunk of sapphire, drifting between a double ultramarine of sky and water. Enter My Blue Fairy Godmother . . .

"Good-now?" she asked.

I didn't know what to say, so just replied: "No, no."

"Why?"

"Well, because I am a sort of negation of it."

"You are very philosophical. 'A negation' is profound talking."

"Is it?"

"If I may broaden the question a bit. If you will—"

"No!"

I will not! And for the next several days, it was purely negative information: The sun shone in the streets, the flame trees brightened the far hills, the deep verandahs shaded the shop windows of the town. A red light. A heavy gust of wind cried out, high-pitched, enraged, "—No!" The freezing negative that those scholared walls had echoed in school, in the afternoons: "Mercy no!"

Moira B.: "Good-*now?*"
Me: "Never!"

My response—and I proceeded assiduously—was negative in nature, prohibitive in intent, and almost entirely sexual: "Nope. Too busy fucking Beverly Hills lawyers."

Self-abnegation is
the higher road.

I prefer not to.

IV

BEING THE AGONIZING ACCOUNT OF MY SORRY STATE FOUR DAYS AFTER THE LETTER & FOUR MONTHS AFTER CATHERINE'S DEPARTURE

There I was as I was before, the empty glass on the table and wanting to cry and feeling like all I felt I wanted was to be away from all this and not have to think any more about any sort of veshch at all: death was the only answer to everything.

And that was it, that was what I viddied quite clear was the thing to do, but how to do it I did not properly know, never having thought of that before, O my brothers. What I wanted was not something violent but something that would make me like just go off gentle to sleep and that be the end of Your Humble Narrator, no more trouble to anybody any more. Perhaps, I thought, if I ittied off to the Public Biblio around the corner I might find some book on the best way of snuffing it with no pain.

So I got the autobus to Center, and it was afternoon now, near two o'clock, as I could viddy from the bolshy Center timepiece. I walked down Marghanita Boulevard and then turned into Boothby Avenue, then round the corner again, and there was the Public Biblio.

It was a starry cally sort of a mesto that I could not remember going into since I was a very very malenky malchick. On all sides, towering bookcases burgeoned with volumes. The floor was amber marble with black basalt trim, a handsome reminder that this building had once been a palace. The furniture was framed in gold and upholstered in satin brocade and it consisted of easy chairs, divans and stools in great variety.

I couldn't remember what it was I wanted at first, then I remembered with a bit of a shock that I had ittied here to find out how to snuff it without pain, so I goolied over to the shelf full of reference veshches. There were a lot of books, but there was none with a title, brothers, that would really do. There were books in Spanish strewn across several tables with mirror tops and cabinets filled with rare and curious things: books of mathematics; books of poets; some of Ovid's fables; all these accursed books of chivalry;* two or three books which one might get a hundred roubles simply for thinking of translating and publishing; a shelf with a row of little green books: a spy novel, a Civil War novel, an ethnology textbook, a study of religion, a book about cancer and one about human genetics; a book about an ape being taught sign language and one about the space race of the 1960s; a book on African public health; the book on French verbs; the book on manipulating the press; a pile of filmbooks: a fantasy filmbook; a filmbook on a small specimen, only one hundred and ten meters long and twenty-two meters in diameter; an old filmbook from before discovery of the spice: *Arrakis: His Imperial Majesty's Desert Botanical Testing Station; The Ways of Arrakis,* imperial filmbook for children; one book weeding out "all the pathological symptoms" of the religious past; Da Vinci's notebook on polemics and speculation; the Chicago phone book; the program from a play; books on religious paintings and cult symbology: *The Symbology of Secret Sects, The Art of the Illuminati, The Lost Language of Ideograms;* books on Crystallography, rare books, books

---

* *Sergas de Esplandian; Amadis of Greece; Don Olivante de Laura; The Garden of Flowers; Florismarte of Hircania; The Knight Platir; The Knight of the Cross; The Mirror of Chivalry; Bernardo del Carpio; Roncesvalles; Palmerin de Oliva; Palmerin of England; Don Belianis; History of the Famous Knight, Tirante el Blanco; Diana; the* ten books of the *Fortune of Love,* written by Antonio de Lofraso, a Sardinian poet; *The Shepherd of Iberia; Nymphs of Henares; The Enlightenment of Jealousy; Pastor de Filida; The Treasury of Various Poems;* the *Cancionero* of Lopez de Maldonado; the *Galatea* of Miguel de Cervantes; the *Araucana* of Don Alonso de Ercilla; the *Austriada* of Juan Rufo, Justice of Cordova; the *Montserrate* of Christobal de Virués, the Valencian poet; *The Tears of Angelica.*

not to be obtained ever again, anywhere; five books in English; the four books of *Amadis of Gaul;* three books of lore; three books on survival in the wilderness; three on guns and shooting—two each on handling medical emergencies, California native and naturalized plants and their uses, and basic living: log-cabin building, livestock raising, plant cultivation, soapmaking—that kind of thing; two books of the *Iliad;* a copy of *A Clockwork Orange;* a copy of Goldstein's book; a copy of a children's history textbook; a whole bookcase of old science fiction novels. Plenty of books for a smart boy to read. There was a medical book that I took down, but when I opened it it was full of drawings and photographs of horrible wounds and diseases, and that made me want to sick just a bit, so then I near cried:

"Nothing is quite right. And the books. The dear old texts. Makes me nervous to see them lined up on the shelves just where they've always been. But they're books, for Chrissake, what am I afraid of?"

A very starry ragged moodge opposite me said:

"What is it, son? What's the trouble?"

"I want to snuff it," I said. "I've had it, that's what it is. Life's become too much for me."

A starry reading veck next to me said: "Shhhh," without looking up from some bezoomny mag he had full of drawings of like bolshy geometrical veshches.

This other moodge said:

"You're too young for that, son. Why, you've got everything in front of you." He pointed out the books in his hands, several shelves of books, a bookcase in the corner and several chairs—all government furniture, of polished yellow wood.

I said nothing.

He went to the table, took up a thick dusty book, opened it. "I have just (let us suppraise) been reading in a (suppressed) book—it is notwithstempting by meassures long and limited—the latterpress is eminently legligible and the paper . . ."

"Fiction," I said. "It's all fiction."

"It's amazing," he said.

"What I've learned I've learned from listening to men talk, not from books."

"Well I mean yes," he said, "don't we all, deep down, you know . . . er . . ." He paused. "We *must* read it."

He eagerly seized upon the big book and flipped over the pages, keeping on wetting his fingers to do this by licking them splurge splurge. He was a bolshy great burly bastard with a very red litso, but he was very fond of myself, me being young and also now very interested in the big book without a title.

"People referred to it, if at all, simply as THE BOOK," he said.

There must be something in books, things we can't imagine, I thought, as I stood there by the gleaming leather volumes.

"Read it to me," he said. He sat down with his elbow on the table, leaned his head on his hand and looked away sullenly, prepared to listen.

"Oh, good God," I said aloud.

But he himself had said that the great open pages resembled Bibles he had seen.

"All right, all right," I said, so I took to reading it closely.

V

BEING THE CONTENTS OF THE BOOK

WHEN THE WORLD WAS NEW, the seven Gods dwelt in harmony, and the races of man were as one people. Belar, youngest of the Gods, was beloved by the Alorns. He abode with them and cherished them, and they prospered in his care. The other Gods also gathered peoples about them, and each God cherished his own people.

But Belar's eldest brother, Aldur, was God over no people. He dwelt apart from men and Gods, until the day that a vagrant child sought him out. Aldur accepted the child as his disciple and called him Belgarath. In the years that followed, others also sought out the solitary God. They joined in brotherhood to learn at the feet of Aldur, and time did not touch them.

Now it happened that Aldur took up a stone in the shape of a cube, carefully rubbed and polished, and he turned the stone in his hand until it became a living box. The power of the living jewel, which men called the Box of Words, was very great, and Aldur worked wonders with it.

Of all the Gods, Torak was the most beautiful, and his people were the Angaraks. They burned sacrifices before him, calling him Lord of Lords, and Torak found the smell of sacrifice and the words of adoration sweet. The day came, however, when he heard of the Box of Words, and from that moment he knew no peace.

Finally, in a dissembling guise, he went to Aldur. "My brother," he said, "it is not fitting that thou shouldst absent thyself from our company and counsel. Put aside this jewel which hath seduced thy mind from our fellowship."

Aldur looked into his brother's soul and rebuked him. "Why dost thou seek lordship and dominion, Torak? Is not Angarak enough for thee? Do not in thy pride seek possession of the box, lest it slay thee."

Great was Torak's shame at the words of Aldur, and he raised his hand and smote his brother. Taking the box, he fled. Since then he has not been heard of.

The centuries rolled past in the lands of the Angarak. Entire civilizations rose and fell while out there those who remained in the Old Empire sat in complacency. New weapons and technologies were spawned. New forms of life. Incident followed upon incident. But no sign of the glowing, embery thing . . . until we had waited a long time and Sir Joshua Byrde, a Turkey merchant, brought it home from Aleppo, and vanished with it a month after he had shown it to the virtuosi, no man knew or knows where.

After seventeen years, it was discovered by an Italian humanist, and lost and rediscovered and sent to Charles, who was in Spain. He sent it in a galley commanded by a French knight named Cormier or Corvere, a member of the Order, but it never reached Spain. You know of Barbarossa, Redhead, Khair-ed-Din? No? A famous admiral of buccaneers sailing out of Algiers then. Well, he took the Knights' galley, took the box, and went to Algiers. That's a fact. That's a fact that the French historian Pierre Dan put in one of his letters from Algiers. He wrote that the box was concealed somewhere in the city for more than a hundred years, until it was carried away by Sir Francis Verney, the English adventurer who was with the Algerian buccaneers for a while.

There's nothing said of the box, it is true, in Lady Francis Verney's *Memoirs of the Verney Family* during the Seventeenth Century. And it's pretty certain that Sir Francis didn't have the box in his clothing somewhere—or the heel of his boot—when he died in a Messina hospital in 1615. But there's no denying the fact that the box did go to Sicily. It was there and it came into the possession there of Victor Amadeus II some time after he became king in 1713.

It turned up next in the possession of a Spaniard who had been with the army that took Naples in 1734—the father of Don José Monino y Redondo, Count of Floridablanca. There's nothing to show that it didn't stay in that family until at least the end of the Carlist War in '40. Then it appeared in Paris at just about the time that Paris was full of Carlists who had had to get out of Spain. One of them must have brought it with him, but, whoever he was, it's likely he knew nothing about its real value. It had been—no doubt as a precaution during the Carlist trouble in Spain—painted or enameled over to look like nothing more than a fairly interesting black box with wires attached. And in that disguise, it was, you might say, kicked around Paris for seventy years of private owners and dealers too stupid to see what it was under the skin.

For seventy years, this marvelous item was, as you might say, a football in the gutters of Paris—until 1911, when a Greek dealer named Charilaos Konstantinides found it in an obscure shop. It didn't take Charilaos long to learn what it was and to acquire it. No thickness of enamel could conceal value from his eyes. Well, Charilaos was the man who traced most of its history and who identified it as what it actually was.

These are facts, historical facts, not schoolbook history, but history nevertheless. In J. Delaville Le Roulx's *Les Archives de l'Ordre de Saint-Jean* there is a reference to it—oblique to be sure, but a reference still. And the unpublished—because unfinished at the time of his death—supplement to Paoli's *Dell' origine ed instituto del sacro militar ordine* has a clear and unmistakable statement of the facts:

> Charilaos had learned the secret of the box. One year to the very day after he had acquired it, I picked up the *Times* in London and read that his establishment had been burglarized and him murdered. I was

in Paris the next day, reached this very apartment, and glanced hastily inside. The box was gone from its place in one of the locked fireproof cases.

Now it makes little difference—they have not yet discovered it—but I should say that at the present time, it is said that a Catholic thickset blond fellow in a brown suit, wearing dark glasses and a rather gay hat—name of Stephen Brooks—might have succeeded in recovering it . . .

VI

BEING A VISUAL REPRESENTATION OF MY THOUGHT PROCESSES AFTER READING SAID BOOK

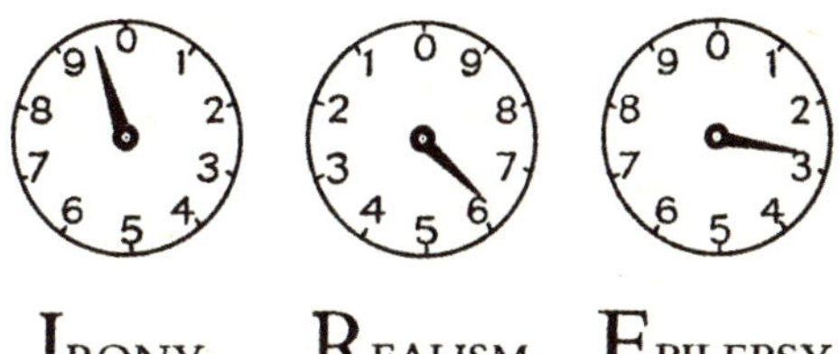

I wish
that there was
a reason to be-
lieve this ~~letter~~
BOOK

- tongue

T.S

I don't know what or who's happening

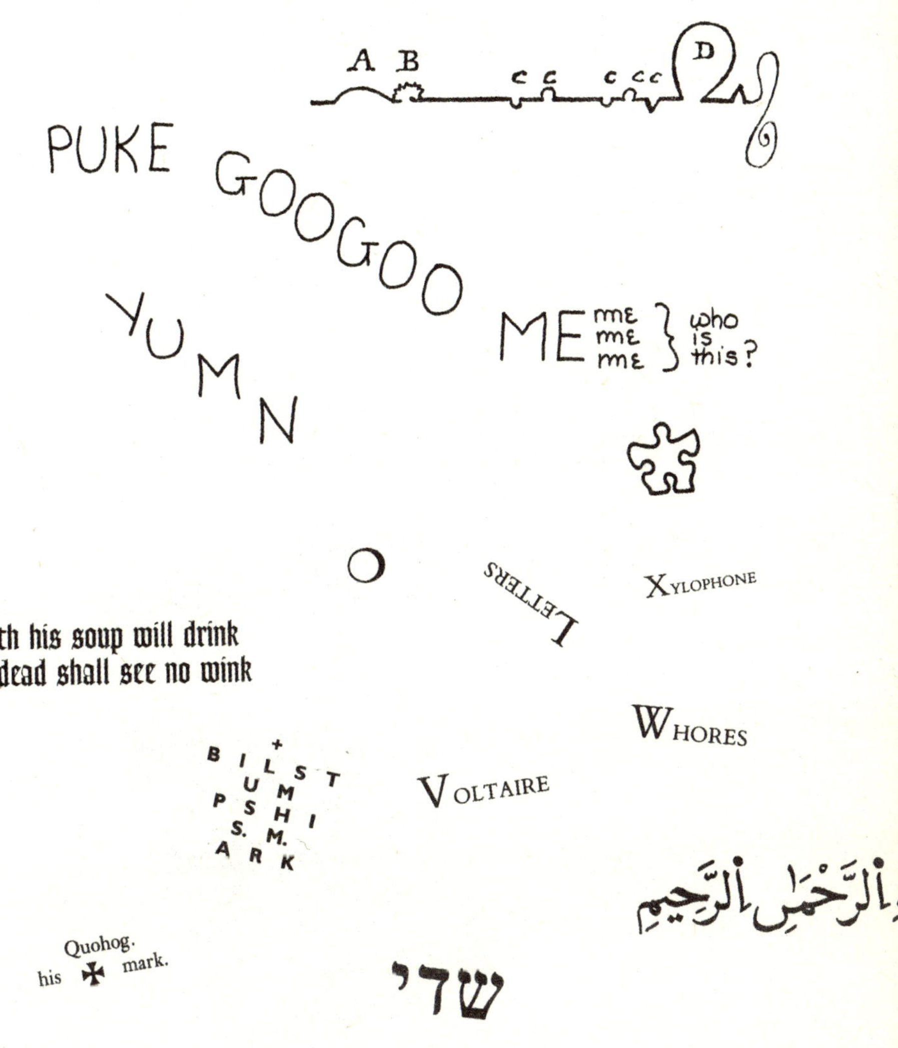

Alas, poor YORICK!

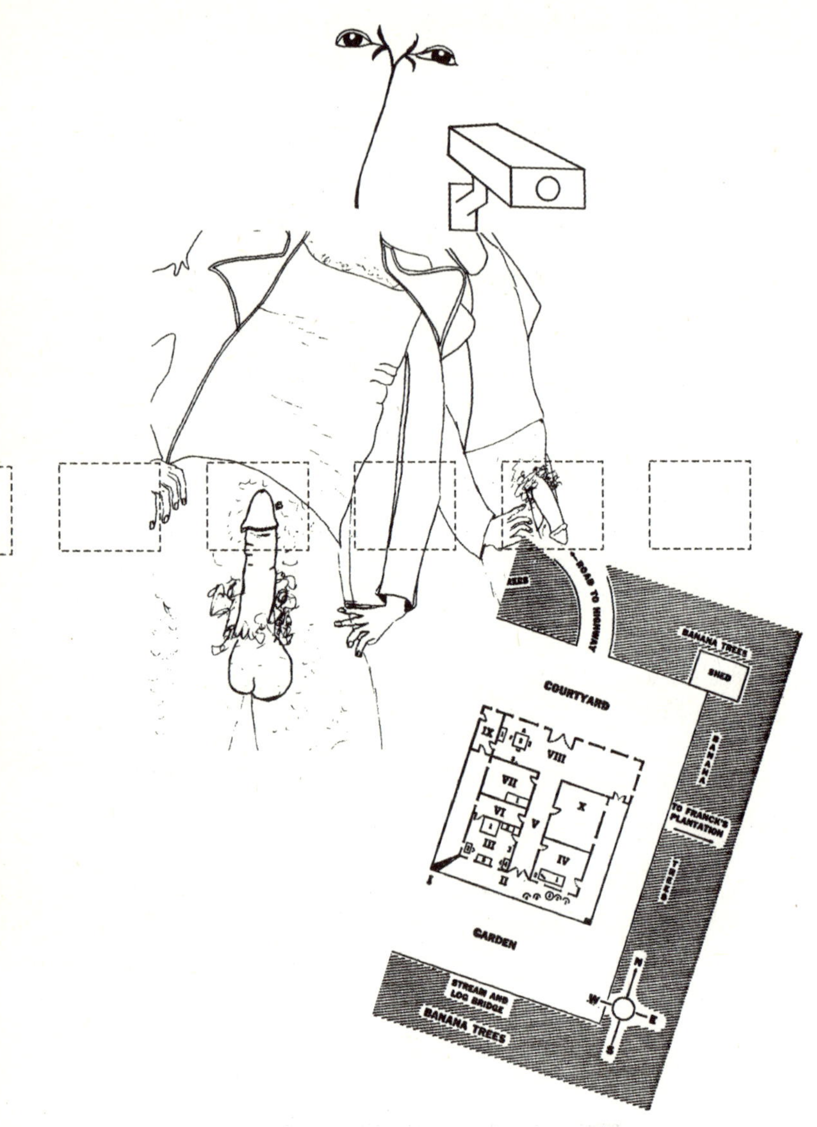

The True Legend of Prince Bladud

and PUBLISHED by his

AUTHORITY.

do blooming | thanks and | you drooping
grew how | do you do you | do blooming
two ma | ma Ma | grew how
two eight | five seven one four | two Miss oh
HARDY,
was killed by a
t of Japan,
T
nory
Empty space
THE LAND OF
E . ything is
the middle of
white cement
spraying out o
of the spray.
the fountain, c
Fifty | two point | two eight | five seven one four
Fifty | two two | two fifty | two point
Fiffee | fiffee fiffee | two tootee | tootee tootee tootee
Hem! | fi | | f

A favorite

OVERTURE

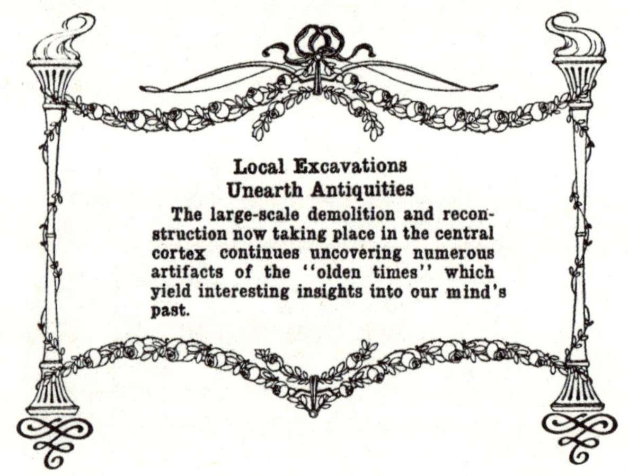

Local Excavations
Unearth Antiquities

The large-scale demolition and reconstruction now taking place in the central cortex continues uncovering numerous artifacts of the ''olden times'' which yield interesting insights into our mind's past.

THIS TABLET
Is erected to his Memory
BY HIS SISTER.

S A T A N
A D A M A
T A B A T
A M A D A
N A T A S*

S A T A N
A D A M A
T A B A T
A M A D A
N A T A S*

The Valley of Love

two	eight	five seven	one four	two	greatgran
two	eight	five seven	one four	two	eight
two	tootee	tootee tootee	pointee	two	eight
Christ!	fi – –	– – – – – – – –	– – – – –	f	phew! ty

beg to inform you that a writ has been issued against you in this suit, in the Court of Common Pleas;[4] and request to know, by return of post, the name of your attorney in London, who will accept service thereof.

We are, Sir,
Your obedient servants,
Dodson and Fogg.

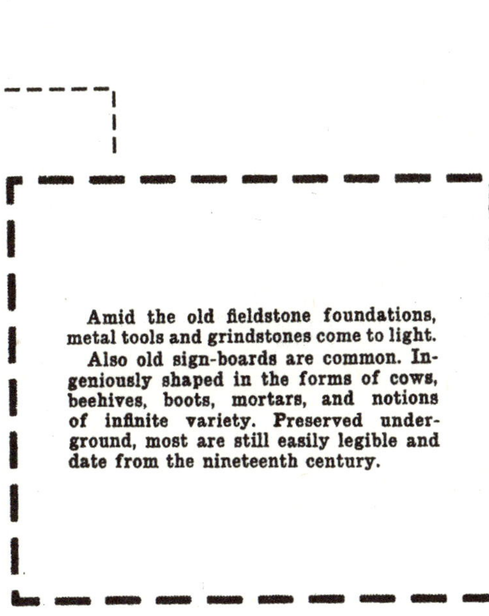

Amid the old fieldstone foundations, metal tools and grindstones come to light.

Also old sign-boards are common. Ingeniously shaped in the forms of cows, beehives, boots, mortars, and notions of infinite variety. Preserved underground, most are still easily legible and date from the nineteenth century.

CARTEPARTI
DE LAMER MEDIT
FAICTE PAR N
FRANÇOÏS OLL
·A·MARSEILL

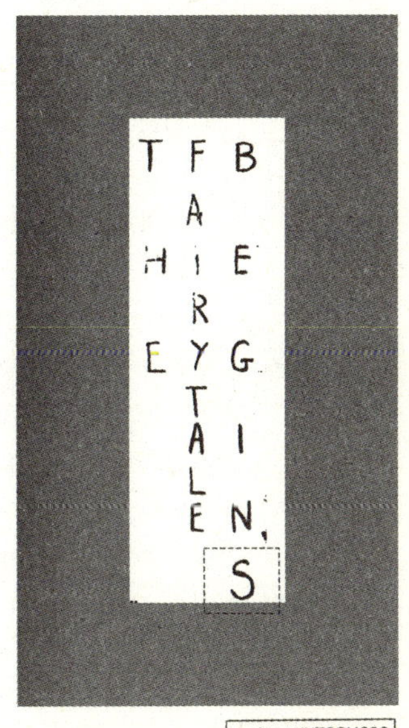

endtransINTCOM626

VII

BEING THE EVENTS OF THE FOLLOWING MORNING TOLD IN THE FORM OF A RUN-ON SENTENCE

The next morning, after having my coffee and planning my strategy of recovering the snuff box, I went to my dressing-room, took two eager strides, and looked out, standing by the window like a man lost in a dream: out in the early morning streets, the small group of runners made its way down University Avenue and turned north on Thirty-Fourth Street: Cassidy ran with a loose stride that approached awkwardness, he chatted quietly with Jerry Mizner and followed the shadowy jogging path to the opposite edge of the park; there, concealed by trees, Count Rugen and four castle guards were rounding a corner, had scarcely turned it when Mr. Serjeant Snubbin appeared, followed by Mr. Mallard and Brother Tadger, closely followed by the Reverend Mr. Stiggins; they passed bushes and trees and ducks in a pond and these farmers running up and down getting up a sweat; the main group, numbering perhaps five, were running toward the gate, the second group included Miss Sally, Mr. Swiveller, and Sampson Bass running uphill, past a block of big homes, fortresses of cement and brick inset with doorways of stained and beveled glass and windows of potted plants, and then halfway up another block, a development built all at once in the Thirties; they ran for a couple of hundred yards through the open space, then the three of them turned and pointed to a wide shoulder on the opposite side of the road; it happened that Kit had been running too and, having the start of them by some few minutes, was a good distance ahead; as they were pretty certain of the road he must have taken, however, and kept on at a great pace, they came up with him, at the very moment when he had taken breath and was breaking into a run again, puffing and blowing; "Stop!" cried Sampson, "Not so fast sir, You're in a hurry?" "Yes, I am," said Kit with so fixed a look of grief and despair in his eyes, he kept running, he was running hard, with occasional little springs, such as a weary man gives who is little accustomed to set any tax upon his legs, as he ran he jerked his hands up and down, waggled his head, and writhed his face into the most extraordinary contortions, "What on earth can be the matter with him?" I asked as I stood in the bow-window looking down the street; my friend rose lazily from his armchair and stood with his hands in the pockets of his dressing-gown, looking over my shoulder, from the window we watched a young man running from house to house, still puffing, still gesticulating, and in an astonishingly short time, minutes only, the street was full of people, disorganized and showing every sign of acute fear, they set off in great haste, some going one way and some another, they seemed to have no definite destination or plan, just the one overwhelming urge to fly from the town; I changed into jogging shorts and a T-shirt, Poirot sat down and looked out the window as Devin, now in a tracksuit, strode across the lot followed by a train of rattled and nettled assistants, they ran around in the big back garden of the Oiie house; "Curious," said Poirot, the nurse opened the door and motioned with her finger for me to come, I followed her into the hall, my mother following me, Poirot followed after her, we had to get down the steps and into the woods to be safe; as I ran down the passage, suddenly everyone was moving, reaching for weapons, John Thorpe came running upstairs, Collet was downstairs in seconds, running toward the back door, Chifoilisk saw him, and followed him, and the servants ran up and downstairs perpetually, they seemed to be running in all directions, and then came the sharp sound of the church bell in the rapid peal of alarm, Cousin Charles hurried up the back steps and across the screened porch into the kitchen, Mother was still there, still wearing the white blouse and the blue high-heeled shoes, she looked at him, and he couldn't read her face, "Run," Charles said, at the front door now, "run, you fool," to which she said, "I have not done much running in the past few years, young man, I see no cause for this hysteria," "Go," he said, "Go, Go," "I—I—Ah, God—" she lunged against the door and half sprang, half fell out, she was on her feet instantly and running, her hair streamed out behind her and she seemed very beautiful, almost goddesslike, and she ran into the luke-warm starburst of a million flashbulbs, June started to cry and ran out of the room, Charles turned on the doorsill to call to Moira B., "Don't try to carry the safe," he said, "put the money in a bag, don't panic," he ran, and we could hear him screaming as he ran toward the village, now behind me, now before me, now on this side, now on that, turned I my affrighted face in the same moment, expecting a furious brother here, armed servants there, and a father armed with terror in his countenance more dreadful than even the drawn sword which I saw or those I apprehended; I ran as fast as he, yet knew not that I ran, my fears adding wings to my feet, thus terrified, I was out of sight of the door in a few minutes, Moira B. held to me with one hand and with the other hand she kept Uncle Julian's shawl across her face, she moved through a world of shades of gray, the muscles in her legs and shoulders ached from the tension, her eyes strained to see, I wondered if Moira B. would slip and fall, running through the light, but we had to get to the woods and there was no other way; on the street I saw a man and a woman, walking toward us, heads bent and their hands on their hats, we ran into a couple of Italians we knew and McAdams, the crowd swirled around them and away; oblivious, we ran as fast as we could—bashed into things, there were screams from the crowd followed by sudden tidelike movement, men and women were tearing across roads and fields, their faces were blank and avid with panic, Moira B. was stumbling, and I wondered if we were going to fall onto the ground in front of them, lying there where they might step on us, then I turned toward the house, running again with Moira B. pulled behind me, and Elbert the grocer and his greedy wife were there, holding their hands to halt us, almost dancing together, and we stopped; I went then to the side, and Jim Donell stepped in front of us, and the main mass of the crowd fled at the sight of him, I took a cautious step, pulling Moira B. a little so that she followed me, suddenly she gave in, worn out, beaten; she was panting, her face was wet, "Claudius?" she said, "Clau-Clau? Tell me, Clau, what do you see? Another world? Can you see all the busy gods running about doing good deeds?" "I guess," I said, gazing absently, she turned on me suddenly, pushed me with a force for which I was unprepared, so that I stumbled back, and she turned and ran back up the road, looking like a modern Atalanta; I stared after her, away to the eastward the distant fires flickered, and now it seemed that here and there houses and barns were burning, most of the doors were wide open in the aftermath of escape, an older man with silvery barbershop hair ran out to the edge of the road, a gray cardigan flapped over his bare chest, and green plaid pants cut off a comical length above his slippers, which were secured to his feet with black electrical tape; six devils congregated on the lawn of a mock Tudor halfway down the street, and they turned at the sound of him, the old man ran fast, veering to arc around them, dark aviator glasses covered his eyes and he had a wireless rig stuck in his ear, into which he narrated his progress, I ran away in a great hurry, all the time, as I now see, I was conscious of extreme terror and my heart was beating as if I had been running for my life, I avoided the most frequented ways and took the most intricate, and thus dashed away through the endless succession of sombre streets, which widened gradually, until I was flying for about a hundred yards or so across a broad balustraded bridge, with the murky river flowing sluggishly beneath, beyond lay another wilderness of bricks and mortar; a dull wrack was drifting slowly across the sky, and light rain drifted between the buildings, the drizzle had deepened into a steady rain by the time I started to get kind of tired, then a cramp set in, pretty soon all I could do was walk, but that cramp really started to get to me, and I had to bend over and hold my side while I kept moving; my face was wet with rain, drops ran down into my mouth, I covered my eyes with my handkerchief, brought myself under control by a violent effort, I looked like a wheezing version of the Hunchback of Notre Dame; as I made my way down the streets, I was not noticed outside, everyone had disappeared into the gloom, the streets were swimming with water, I was breathless, bruised all over and soaking wet, but I felt triumphant, I ran, digging my fingers into my gut to stifle the pain, I ran all the way from Plains Street along the East Road, and without halting turned up the Bywater Road, which ran for some way sloping up between high banks of the river, going north, round a bend, along a furlong from the main road, I saw a runner far ahead of me moving at a rapid clip, fast enough that I'd lose sight of him in bends; I thought he was wearing a sleeveless white singlet, warm-ups, and a headband, but he kept disappearing and reappearing, and anyway, then he turned into a tongue of trees and bushes where I couldn't see him anymore, and I knew what the loneliness of the long-distance runner felt like, realizing that as far as I was concerned this feeling was the only honesty and realness there was in the world and knowing it would be no different ever, no matter what I felt, and no matter what anybody else tried to tell me; slipping and stumbling, I observed that a weight of despair and remorse pressed on my heart, which nothing could remove, and yet—and yet—and yet somehow, it seemed a snuff box—it seemed almost ludicrous—the box would be the answer, would seem perfectly plain in the end, and thus life would be a merrier business with that little harmless box.

VIII

BEING AN ACCOUNT OF THE SOMETHING THAT WAS OUT THERE

The afternoon rained on. Lightning quivered faintly on the verge of the horizon and was the only sight that varied the dull gloom in which everything was wrapped. Then, ere the great dark came upon. All was indeed changed; the frowning mountains seemed fading away, and the time seemed interminable, for the rolling clouds obscured the moon. All was in dead, grim silence, as if in terror of the worst.

Suddenly a noise roused my hearing. What was it? A blast of wind? A presence above and beyond that of humankind? I began to fear—horrible fears; but then came to me some trick of the moonlight, some weird effect of shadow; but I kept looking, and it could be no delusion: within a very short distance of Bow Street, there had been a sudden, slight movement. A shadowy form moved swiftly through the gloom and disappeared.

"Something's out there," I hissed.

"Where?" someone shouted from a few yards behind.

I whirled around.

A seven-foot-tall man leaned casually against a crypt. He was dressed in a tight-fitting pinstriped suit, purple vest, and white shirt. A top hat perched on his head and a smoking cigar dangled from his mouth. His face was painted to look like a skull.

The speaker was Harrison. Having been one of the living, one of the dead, and now one of the living dead, he had seen himself as the ultimate sophisticate. He had assumed that the world held nothing new for him, had nothing to teach him. Now this: the falling rain churned the puddles, and something out there was calling him—calling him away from the grave, and the gray, dead waste of the Barren.

"You're being mysterious." I frowned.

"Believe me, it isn't intentional," he replied. "I don't know much more than you do. I'm just hoping we'll know it, whatever it is, when we see it."

Something caught my attention, off to our right . . .

"An animal?"

"No, there aren't any animals that size. Probably one of our people meditating."

"What, at this hour?"

"God takes calls around the clock."

I swallowed, my mouth oddly dry. "I have the feeling . . . something's out there . . . bear, perhaps."

We peeped quietly over the tops of the bushes.

"Something bad," Harrison finally agreed. "Okay. If you'll follow me, please . . . ?"

The rain suddenly began to fall harder than before. The wind picked up, too, as we crossed the square then trudged along the edge to the house where he had lived for almost two years.

On the threshold of the house, I shook my head sharply. Fatigue depression, I told myself—it was nothing more than that. A raw uneasiness. Then I thought I heard something out there like—like a low splashing. A whisper. A crackle. The hair on the neck prickled. A rustle in the bushes out there at the end of the house.

Harrison looked as if he had seen something. "Something out there," he said, pointing into the fog.

He headed for the front door. It stood ajar, and looked as if it could never close all the way. It scraped across grit on the floor as he forced it open. "Anyone here?" he asked. But the building's insides swallowed his voice.

The interior was as dark as a cave. At one end were two bunks built against the wall. In the middle of the room stood a rough table of slabs and in a corner was a rusty stove propped up with bricks in lieu of missing legs.

A babel of voices burst forth at our approach. "Hello? Hey!" "Don't yell. It might—" "Who is it?" "Hello? Are you all right?" "Come on!" "Hello? You hurt?" "I'm Randon Kelsey-Ramos of the Carillon Group." "I'm Jonas Nyebern. I'm a doctor." "Heather." "Toby." "Melanie." "Ted!" "Ned Blake, great-grandson of old Josiah Blake." "Who's out there now?" "It's . . . it's a . . . there's a—" "No, if it's a sneaking lion, I can manage to kill him, but—" "Your eyes are haunted." "You see something?" "Who are you, what the hell do you want!?"

"You know who I am," Harrison said. "I'm afraid I come with the house."

"Is there really something out there?" That was Gerstan, bouncing up alongside me.

"Yes, you can see it seems to move up and down in puddles, and in the torrents."

"Something's always out there for all of us," Giles said. "It's just that most people don't realize that."

"And I know there's good evidence to support the fact that something's out there, because too many prophecies come true," Calandra said sharply, peering into the darkness.

Ned spoke quietly, but his gray eyes were blazing. "You think something's out there, eh?" he began in a voice that betrayed his suppressed excitement, "I found something out there at the end of the house!"

"What was it?"

"It was a footprint!" He could not keep back the break that was in his breath.

"Yeah, I saw a hundred of 'em," drawled Jonas. "Half the dance crowd walked all over that stretch—"

"The footprint I saw wasn't made by a dancing shoe . . ." replied Ned.

Giles looked alarmed.

"I'm scared," Toby said. A blast of wind skirled under the back porch roof, as shrill as an electronic shriek, as questing and insistent as a living creature.

Heather crouched at Toby's side. "We'll be okay, honey. Now that we know something's out there, we'll handle it."

She wished she could be half as confident as she sounded.

"Probably a raccoon or something," Eric said and took two steps to the window.

Harrison was still staring beyond the rain-spotted window, as if oblivious of Jonas and Eric. His eyes were not focused on the window sill, on nothing so close as that, but on some distant point in the stormy night.

Tionne crowded in next to them, and together they peered through the window. A breath of wind soughed round the walls—hush—sh—sh; a loose window pane let in a tiny draught.

Harrison was murmuring something . . . something important. Suddenly a noise roused his attention.

"Why, there *is* something out there—sounded like people calling," he again whispered.

Melanie stood very still, though a little uneasy.

Ted hurried over and shut off the boom box. Everything was quiet.

The sudden quiet was jarring, eerie. Except for the crackle of the fire and the steady breath of the rain, there wasn't a sound.

Then there was.

A howl that was almost a scream broke the silence. And then——
Snap! Crunch!

Melanie grabbed Ted's arm, hard.

A rustling and another twig breaking.

"Something's out there," Ted whispered. "It's . . ." Before he could finish, a low growl came, instantly followed by a violent thrashing in the brush.

"I'm going to take a look," Ted whispered.

He got down a low-burning lantern from where it hung, turned it up, and then he went out and closed the door behind him. As he did so, the mournful wail was still going, rising, falling, rising again.

Ted walked cautiously, shakily, toward the sound, just now falling away. "Hello?" His form was dim, broken into segments by the shadows.

"Ted! Come back here! I'm scared!" Melanie said.

He turned to look back, his face illumined like a lone planet in the dark of space. "Can you see anything?" he said.

We could only see his face and his right shoulder.

Just beyond his right shoulder, two silvery-green retinas turned into the light.

"Ted, run! Run!" Melanie screamed the scream of her life, backing away, hands to her face.

Ted spun around just in time to take a blow to his head that nearly snapped his neck. He tumbled like a rag doll out of sight.

"Ted!"

Very few people were not focused on the window; curiosity fought panic and pain.

"What in hell is it?"

Colin paused beside me. "Something worse than you ever dreamed of. We've got to get out of here before it finds us."

Charlie grunted.

I sighed and looked back at Colin.

"The thing just killed something out there," he yelled at Charlie Trask. "It's coming this way. Are you going to sit there and—"

"No such varmint in these kays," old Charlie said.

"Something's out there killing!" The voice was Zack's. "Get out!"

Colin radiated tension as he stood beside me. "Let's get to the Paranorm Center. Now."

I nodded.

Colin and I ran.

IX

BEING THE SIBILANT SOUNDS OF OUR RESTLESS RACE THROUGH THE WOODS, PAST THE LAKE, BACK INTO THE WOODS, THROUGH THE FIELDS, OVER HILLS, AND TO MY COMPANION'S EVENTFUL ENCOUNTER WITH THE BEAST

ARREEYAAAH! EEEEEK! GRROWR! RRAAAAUUUGGHHH! IT'S GROWING—COMING TOWARDS US! WHAT? NO! NO! GET AWAY! GET AWAY FROM ME! SKR-II-ICK! AAAGH-HHH! HOLY CROW! WHAT WAS THAT? NYAWRRRRR! WHA—WHAT WAS THAT? I'LL TELL YOU WHAT IT WASN'T! IT WAS NO PRACTICAL JOKER! IT'S NO GAG! THIS IS THE REAL THING! YUHROOWR ROAARRNK . . . AND THEN . . . ARRAWRRR! THAT SOUND . . . THAT, HORRIBLE SOUND! LIKE A BEAST BREATHING HEAVILY! HUNNH! HUNH! HUNH! HUNNH! SLURP! SLAP! SLURP! A CRY THAT WOULD CHILL HUMAN BONES! AVROOO AAROOO A—A FREAK CREATURE OF SOME KIND! RUM-MMMPHHTTTT! EEEEEYAAHH! A M-MONSTER! GNNARRRR LOOK AT THE THING! A MONSTER—AND—THAT SHIRT—IT'S UNCLE DAVOS'S! HE HAS KILLED UNCLE DAVOS! AND IT'S—IT'S COMING STRAIGHT FOR ME! HAVE TO TAKE TO THE WOODS . . . EE-YAAOOWW GRAWRRRR LOOK OUT! HRROOGA! CRREAK! OH NO—HE FOUND ME! GWARR-R-R! NO! COME BACK! DON'T LEAVE ME—ALONE! NNG-YAWRR! ARROOO! WHAT ARE YOU SAYING? I DON'T UNDERSTAND A WORD! NO! STOP! ARRRGGGGH! BVDFTRW SPKTQUX MNKLRZU! WHAT THE DEVIL DO YOU THINK—ARRRGH! SOMETHING'S HAPPENING TO ME! NEE-Y-DIP-NEE-Y-D. SUDDENLY . . . RR-AAGHH! BA-WAK! WAIT A MINUTE—SOMETHING'S GONE WRONG! GOOD GRIEF!*

* "—We can't let you live to warn the world! You know too much!"

HE ISN'T FOOLING! RYRAWRR! AAA-ROOW! WHAAP! O-OH! MEE-YAA! MEE-YAA! AARRROOOOOO IT-IT'S ALIVE . . . AND IT'S ATTACKING ME! . . . BUT . . . HOW IS IT POSSIBLE? UUUUUUUUUUUUUU OH NO—! KREEUNCH! GRAWR-R-R! THEN DIE, FOUL CREATURE! BWAAAAAA! WHAT WAS THAT? LIKE THE CRIES OF TEN-THOUSAND BABES! NOW—DIE, YOU CHILD OF THE DEVIL! UNNGHH! WHOOSH! EEYOOWWR! BUT WHAT KEPT IT ALIVE? EEYAWWRRR! EYAWWRRRR! YAAROOO!

X

BEING THE TWO ROUTES BEFORE ME AT THIS FIGURATIVE FORK IN THE ROAD

A

You choose the past.

You decide not to risk it.

You just watch what happens.

You hide from view.

You say, "Because I want to be back with my family and friends."

You say, "Because I don't want to take a chance of being in a bad time."

You decide to start back home.

You take one last look.

You wave goodbye to your friend.

You run.

You return to the hill and try to find your way back.

You follow a wide path.

B

You choose the future.

You remain with your new friend.

You shake your head, wondering what you'll do.

You close your eyes to gather your wits and strength.

You decide to take your chances with the giant.

You say, "I'll do it."

You prepare to fight.

You try to run past.

You swing the bottle at the figure.

You run over to your friend.

You say, "Let's go now."

Your friend, running right at the monster: "You!"

You say, "No!"

You soon find an animal trail leading through the dense undergrowth, through forests and along rivers and streams.

You try to make it across the bridge.

You trudge on into town, where the innkeeper lets you have a room for the night.

The next morning you get a ride on a coach back home.

You decide to stay at home.

You say you'll accept a life of perpetual pleasure.

You do.

The End

Your friend from the past is gone, dissolved it seems, into the jaws of the monster.

You try to get away.

You spy the entrance to a cave under a rock ledge.

You run for the cave.

You enter the cave.

You hear a terrible grinding, crunching noise.

You miss the company of your friend.

You take the first tunnel.

You follow the right branch.

You hear a deep-throated growl.

You follow the left branch.

You take a tunnel further on.

You try to follow the wall of the cave.

You go up to the wall.

You see an opening in the ground.

You try to swim through the underwater tunnel.

You find yourself gasping for breath.

You decide to turn back.

You take the tunnel leading to the left.

You hear a sound up ahead.

You take the tunnel leading to the right.

You try one of the tunnels as a way out.

You run out of the cave.

You continue on.

You brave the freezing wind.

You insist on pushing on.

You decide to take the dragon trail.

You decide to go through No Man's Forest.

You leave.

You continue on through the clearing.

You seek shelter.

You go to the farm.

You walk up to the opening door.

You call out—"Hello."

You ask for refuge.

You ask Jervis to let you inside the house.

You go through the swinging door into the dining room.

You say, "Who are you?"

You speak to Mrs. B.

You decide to humor Mrs. B and have some cheese and crackers.

You decide to risk eating some mushrooms.

You agree to rest.

You say "yes."

You follow her out of the room.

You go back to the front hall.

You call to the cat to show you are friendly.

You start up the stairway.

You go up the stairs.

You try to sleep until morning.

Go on to the next page.

XI

BEING THE CONTINUATION OF COLUMN B

Around the beginning of breakfast time, I woke up with a belligerent defiance, though I barely registered why. Soft blue light filled the bedroom: Bottles on the table beside the bed. Blue and white bed. My boots, breeches, and belt at the bottom of the bed. I barely glanced at these. I blew out breath and could see it below. I blew out another breath and I began to realize it had been the booze last night: like in the Beach Boys song. A bad vibration. Mrs. B!

I bent forward and then decided if I bent over that far, my head might burst out on both sides. So I brought a bottle of Bevo into my mouth, with a hideous burping sound. I breathed shallowly and bitterly. Better. And now I began to smell the able-bodied aromas I have associated with bakeries since I was a boy—bread and butter, bagels and sizzling bananas—and struggled out of bed, bumping into stuff: the bedside lamp, the broad couch with blue silk, the cushioned benches, the bureau with its beauty. The bedroom door was ajar and for a brief moment I couldn't bring myself to budge it. I was very badly bereft of speech, and my mind kept beating hard. Thunder boomed in my body. My eyeballs contracting, sending a brief shiver up my back. In the living room Bunter's bell gave a dim little shake. "Water's still warm, bagels still blazing." I reached out and pushed the bedroom door suddenly back.

It was the bedecked second story of a brick bungalow, a place of baby-carriages, rubber balls, a mesh bag of glass balls, and a Family Bible. All about the Bible—breakthrough book here. Looking at it brought back the last dream of the night before:

> Bad weather was blowing up the Bellevue Avenue Hill, over a black land of hard little bungalows, small, but brave with brick walls. Beyond them was a spangly burst of blue with the bang travelling far behind, and there was a jerky breeze blowing around. The whole Bellevue district seemed broken. How could this be? Had always been the best: blocks of wooden, beautiful bungalows, a business-building, and bikes. On those endless four blocks something bade me go back to the bar. "Bill's not here," Berenice said seriously. She stood at the barrier, blocking the bonniest bevy of beauteous bathing babes in burlesque. I balked and walked back and saw the blue shapes: the tax boys, boot to boot, blocking our way back to the Busy Folks' Bible Class. The Boosters cheered, they bawled back. They threw a lot of balls. One a soft blue. I picked it up and ran the ball of my thumb over, bemused. Then the thunder boomed and the rain began again, but I barely registered. It was revenge, like a boiling flood of molten butter, I betokened. "That big dream must be given up," Berenice said, throwing her broad bare arms both ways.

Remembering what Berenice had said brought me out of this bedtime daze and back home to this little bungalow, the bright light coming in the blue window above the broken bottle. I hadn't realized how bizarre this beautiful house could be.

I bounced on downstairs. Ben Berkey blinked and looked at Bunter, then bemoaned: "Who's before me?" Bunter looked glassily back at me with a bleary flavor of unbelief. No sign of Mrs. B.

"*Who's before me?*" Ben Berkey burst out and bellowed at me.

I looked at him with brief but oh so clear—because the brain—surprise. "Well, come on, brother! One of the livest banquets that has recently been pulled off occurred last night in our beautiful bungalow. There was a beautiful musical background. I heard a washtub bass, brass bell, bagpipes. In another bit the sound of breaking glass; someone began to bang a tambourine."

"Oh boy."

"Mrs. B and I talked a long, long time about blockheads, brutes, and even a stupid brat like you." I said no more, blinked twice.

"Brats? *Blockheads?* I believe that is a bad word," he babbled.

"Bad words were made for bad things," I blinked.

"I wish we could break a leg," Ben whispered, for he was a bashful man, when suddenly from behind us sprang out Mrs. B, awakened with bare hands.

"Why, Ted dear," Mrs. B said. I felt a start at my botched name coming from her bumbling mouth, but it was only momentary, before she said, "Make your way to breakfast." I began to hurry back a few brief words, but she was gone, bouncing into the buttery.

Both of the men began to back up briefly. "Sorry, Teddy, buddy." "You've got me bare hands." "Just followin the boss's orders." "I remember you, buddy." "No bad."

I moved forward, blowing like the big bad wolf. I went into the bathroom, wanting to get rid of the sweat on my body before breakfast. After a brief bubble bath, I breezed into the kitchen, gazed at all three Baudelaire children and Ben Berkey—greeting the occupants boisterously—bounced triumphantly across the bench, and enlightened Mrs. B on the battlefields of Berkeley, the barrenness of Bellevue, the Boosters and their belongings. But the brutally pressing matter was breakfast. A pint of berries had been sprinkled busily on top of each bowl. Beaming at each of the Baudelaire youngsters, Mrs. B said abstractedly, ". . . but perhaps with a bit of butter and bread, the Baudelaire troubles had begun to break up . . ." Then her eyes bulged: "By golly, that's the best and worthiest blackberry." She held the unwavering belief that those berries were the blackest black, and the bushes bending with their burden in the backyard were brought from Berlin.

"But the best berries were from Boston!" said Ben Berkey. But it was B who had the splendidly blatant applause from the brethren.

She turned on the bubble seat and murmured in lyric beatitude, "By golly, I guess you've had some bad beginning yourself, Ben . . ."

"Bad beginning!?" Ben bit.

"Reason she's got Ben beaten is because she has got SOME brains!" said Burrell.

Ben bounced from his chair, grabbed his bifocals and looked at the brethren and beyond, into the backyard. "By a vote I'd better you, bastards!"

She, Mrs. B, both leading the brethren and being bored: "By golly, if that isn't blaspheming!"

The boys condescended, bumped into Ben as if bullets would have bounced off; boot to boot, blocking whenever Ben began to back up. Ben began to beg. He held up both hands as his bruised balls no doubt tried to climb back inside his body.

I began to believe this business was boring. When Ben, that old blabbermouth, began to believe his business—that blaa—was my business also, I blew out breath and bellowed my bit: "Beautiful bungalow, breakfast, bread and butter, Mrs. B." And, while the little brigade was still at breakfast, I breezed up to the bedroom and briefly packed the new briefcase that the boy, the Baudelaire youngster, betrothed to me. While you were busy reading books about bedrooms at the back of bungalows and the bedside belongings the bedrooms beheld, I was barely beginning to fill the briefcase without a word about bedrooms at the back of bungalows and the bedside belongings the bedrooms beheld when I backed into the wall, bumped into the table beside the bed, and the bedside lamp bounced off.

"Oh boy," I said with big eyes. I bent over the broken edges and began to crawl with a very brisk motion towards broken glass. "That's bizarre," I said, brushing by the blood that the broken edges bled on my body, and then beheld a basket. I found a box hiding behind the basket under the bed, a box with the word "Brooks" printed on the back.

I stood up, yanked the box with bold patterns written on the front. A cobweb hung from the bottom of the box. I thought of checking the bottom of the box for bearing evil tidings, then decided to put it back under the bed.

"Now, by golly, if that isn't pretty," a voice sighed before the baronial fireplace. It laughed a brazen, smoke-broken laugh.

I bent forward in an utter panic, beheld a trim, blue-coated figure: Mrs. B!

With amiable belligerence, she began to speak, dropping an involuntary little glance at the box I was holding in both hands.

XII

BEING THE CONTINUATION OF THE CONTINUATION OF COLUMN B

She had found the box in an antiques barn, she said simply, "after what happened to Floyd."

"Floyd? Thursby?" I asked.

She nodded, hissed, "Yes," in a hushed voice.

I took the box and studied it with big round eyes. The circular top of the box was ornamented with a circle of small colorless pearls, but an object of this size?

"It's a fake," I said hoarsely. "And you know that the real one, now, is a small object. If I do not capture it, many bad things will happen."

"That's why I haven't it now. I'm afraid to touch it except to turn it over to somebody else right away."

"All right," I growled, stepping into her face. "You've had your little joke. Now tell us about it. Are you ready to tell us what you have done with the box?"

B. smiled and said: "But I haven't got the snuff box."

"Then where is it?" I inquired.

"Where Catherine has been."

I nearly died of surprise and horror. "Miss Catherine? Catherine! She's my wife!"

She nodded.

"It can't be right. It can't be."

She nodded.

"It can't be right," I kept repeating over and over again. "Name! Name! It can't be right." With all my nerves in a tingle, I gave a cry. It was an insane, impassioned, wild cry—the cry of a vixen shot through the body—it flew into another room and pointed everywhere by the sounds of the day. It began fading and died away in a moment.

She nodded. "With Catherine."

"And you know where that is?"

"I don't know. I didn't miss the box until yesterday. I should not have missed it then, except that a man in Los Angeles named Morningstar called up, said he was a dealer, and was the Box of Words, as he called it, for sale?"

"You are a liar."

"I *am* a liar," she said. "I have always been a liar."

"Don't brag about it. It's childish." I was pained, for I knew how keenly Holmes would know where she is—he told me of Catherine's illness about six weeks before.

I came out from between table and bench. "Was there any truth at all in that yarn?"

She hung her head. Dampness glistened on her dark lashes. "Some," she whispered.

"How much?"

"Not—not very much. It *is* stolen, it must be recovered without delay."

"How would it be stolen?" I asked.

"By anyone in this house, very easily. The keys are in my bag, and my bag lies around here and there. It would be a very simple matter to get hold of the keys long enough to unlock a door and then return the keys. Difficult for an outsider, but anybody in the house could have stolen it."

"I see. How do you establish that Catherine had taken the box?"

"I don't—in a strictly evidential sense. But I'm quite sure of it. The servants are three women who have been here many, many years—long before

I married Stephen Brooks, which was only seven years ago. The gardener never comes in the house. I have no chauffeur, because either my son or my secretary drives me. My son didn't take it, first because he is not the kind of fool that steals from his mother, and secondly, if he had taken it, he could easily have prevented me from speaking to Morningstar. Miss Davis—ridiculous. Just not the type at all. Too mousy. No, Miss Catherine is the sort of lady who might do it just for spite, if nothing else."

"No signs of a burglar, I suppose? It would take a pretty smooth worker to lift just one valuable snuff box, so there wouldn't be. Maybe I had better look the room over, though."

She said calmly, "Maybe you'd better not," and showed me the thing (an ugly-looking magazine pistol), and she told me it was impossible. "Don't attempt anything rash, Mr. . . ."

I looked at the gun in her hand. It was aimed at my heart.

XIII

BEING THE CONTINUATION OF THE CONTINUATION OF THE CONTINUATION OF COLUMN B

You speak sharply to Mrs. B.

You try to reason with her.

You try to make up a believable story.

You insist you are telling the truth.

You say, "Because I want to be back with my family and friends!"

You scream for help.

You prepare to fight.

You do.

You wrench yourself away.

You try to run past her.

You try to escape out one of the front windows.

You decide to climb out the window, jump to the roof, and then find your way down from there.

You close your eyes to gather your wits and strength.

You hang on.

You jump.

You jump down on the wooly mammoth.

You jump to the ground.

You follow the cat.

You say, “Let’s go now.”

You run.

You continue through the clearing.

You head west.

You run down the road only until you are out of sight of the cottage, and then you say, “There, the curse is ended.”

Go on to the next page.

XIV

BEING THE ACCURATE ACCOUNT OF HOW I PASSED THE TIME AFTER MY TUMULTUOUS TIFF AT MRS. B'S

The sun was up so high that I judged it was after eight o'clock. I laid there in the grass and the cool shade thinking about things. Several minutes passed. I was conscious of little, save a sensation of cold and hopelessness and fear. So, when Ralph Denham appeared—my man of four watches, larboard, starboard, dog or dath—I was very glad.

"Howday you doom?" he said to me in a sharp whisper.

"There's no 'go,' no life in me at all these days. I am like a clock with a broken spring."

"Not broken, my boy;" urged the other, "only run down. Try and see if we can't wind you up a bit."

I nodded to show that I had heard, asked him if he would mind telling me something, "Why, my good feller, do you know what o'clock it is—" glanced at his watch and saw that it was past nine o'clock. "Good heavens! nine o'clock! I must get to Holmes's by noon!"

Denham went on quickly, called the carriage, and we set off, went at a rate of a league and a half an hour, as near as I could guess.

At ten o'clock we started to see that forty-five minutes had somehow slipped by since he had come. By eleven o'clock, the atmosphere of concentration was running so strongly in one direction that any thought of a different order could hardly have survived its birth more than a moment or so. Twenty-two minutes after eleven we cleared the lower slopes of the mountains. Twenty-nine minutes after eleven, a.m., my companion noiselessly got up, took his hat in his left hand, put it on his head with an automatic motion. 11:30 a.m. we came to the village.* And it was eleven thirstytoo befour we had passed the H— border and begun to admire the scenery. I thought for a second, "In the sky a white clockface drifts conveniently by." At any rate, whatever were my wanderings, the clock chimed twelve as I entered the house. The noon whistle blew. The others departed. At 12:02 p.m., my life changed forever.

At that moment, I remember, tinny and choked with static, the distinctive sound of John Fogerty's Creedence Clearwater Revival band came out of the speaker. The song ended and the disc jockey came on. "Yeah, that's Creedence. And speakin of bad moon, it looks like it may be risin over before long. The Fearless Forecaster says high pressure will give way by one o'clock this afternoon to a widespread low-pressure area which is just gonna grind to a stop in our area. Temperatures will fall rapidly, and precipitation should start around four o'clock, or five at the latest."

The whole village was suddenly electrified by the ghastly news. The tale flew from man to man, from group to group, from house to house. It was only six minutes past twelve.

For the better part of an hour, I waited in the drawing room. Mr. Alan Sykes walked into the little room for a drink at twenty minutes past twelve. He helped himself to a gin. Byron ate lunch, the silver watch open beside him. About half noon, click o'clock, pip emma, Grinwicker time, by your querqcut quadrant, the others departed. Boy, I sat till around one o'clock or so, getting drunk as a bastard. I could hardly see straight. But ten minutes of one o'clock Sherlock Holmes returned from his excursion. I had to look three times before I was certain that it was indeed he.

---

* I remember the village is called Morality. There you will find a very judicious gentleman whose name is Mr. Legality. It was almost twelve o'clock when he emerged onto the street. He came into sight looking at his watch. Then he looked at a municipal clock in the courthouse tower and then at the sun, with an expression of exasperation and outrage.

"I have seen your missus. Like the queenoveire," said Holmes when he had closed the door behind him.

"Catherine?" I cried hurriedly.

"Catherine," he repeated.

"Where is Miss Catherine?" I demanded sternly, supposing I could frighten him into giving intelligence, by catching him thus, alone.

He straightened himself out and began the following remarkable statement, looking at his watch from time to time: "Catherine came to me, one morning, at eight o'clock, and said she was that day an Arabian merchant, going to cross the Desert with caravan; and I must give her plenty of provision for herself and beasts: a horse, and three camels, personated by a large hound and a couple of pointers. Then she said that she had been in the Piazza since eight o'clock the previous evening collecting material. Then she told me about some other guy, some West Point cadet, that was cutting his throat over her too."

"Big deal." I swallowed and tried to listen.

Holmes nodded. "I told her to meet me under the clock at the B—at two o'clock, and not to be late, because the show probably started at two thirty &c. At 2:00 p.m., I ran along the North Terrace, but could see no sign of the white figure which I expected. Around 2:15 at least fifteen persons witnessed me as if my feet were weighted with lead. I still waited for a while, then I made my way to the main lounge. Its timepiece marked 2:30. At three o'clock p.m., and soon after four, I stood at the foot of the sign-post of W—, waiting the arrival of the coach which was to take her to meet me. But it was never to be recovered. We had been walking ever so peacefully down a long blind alley at 8 o'clock that morning, but that was our end."

There was a pause. The ticking of the clock began to bring itself into notice.

"That's all?" I said.

For a moment or two he looked very sad, and said in a sort of far-away voice, as though saying it rather to himself than to me:—"All over!

all over! I did not know what to do. I did not dare return to the apartment which I inhabited, but felt impelled to hurry on, although wetted by the rain, and discovered to my sleepless and aching eyes the church of I—, its white steeple and clock, which indicated the sixth hour. At that hour I learned that Mr. Bloxam had seen Startop who had called at eleven o'clock to speak to my father, and had found out what I wanted to know: The Gibraltar ship wouldn't do for Catherine; it passed the Tagus in the morning—nearly 10:00 a.m.—and Cape St. Vincent shortly after sunset. The Tangier ship, a slow old tub with one class only, was more suitable. It passed the Tagus between 9 p.m. and midnight."

"And afterwards!?" prompted I.

His hand closed like a vise upon my wrist in his agitation. "Afterwards? Nothing afterwards. All I know for certing . . ." said Holmes. ". . . I think that this typewritten letter is from her." He revealed a sheet of blue paper, scrawled over with notes and figures.

As soon as the small clock of my courage should have ticked out the right second, I transferred my eyes straight to the little passage, which contained the following memoranda:

Reached Paris, Thursday, October 3rd, at 7.20 a.m.
Left Paris, Thursday, at 8.40 a.m.
Reached Turin by Mont Cenis, Friday, October 4th, at 6.35 a.m.
Left Turin, Friday, at 7.20 a.m.
Arrived at Brindisi, Saturday, October 5th, at 4 p.m.
Sailed on the 'Mongolia,' Saturday, at 5 p.m.
Reached Suez, Wednesday, October 9th, at 11 a.m.

"These dates," said Holmes quietly; "were inscribed in an itinerary divided into columns, indicating the month, the day of the month, and the day for the stipulated and actual arrivals at each principal point—Paris, Brindisi, Suez, Bombay, Calcutta, Singapore, Hong Kong, Yokohama,

San Francisco, New York, and London—from the 2nd of October to the 21st of December, 11.40 a.m.; and giving a space for setting down the gain made or the loss suffered on arrival at each locality. This methodical record thus contained an account of everything needed—"

"Where is she now?" I interrupted. "Still you have not told me."

He looked dreadfully white and, with the pungent cleanly smell of hydrochloric acid, told me that he had seen our young lady this very morning eleven o'clock, hurrying towards the nearest station: "A sheet of note-paper fell on the ground. I ran into the yard to catch it. She had less choice than the sun, so she ordered the carriage which had been hired for the occasion. She had scribbled *Jack Straw's Castle, ten o'clock* at the top of the paper."

When Sherlock Holmes looked at his watch, it was still shortly before one o'clock. The last train to S— left shortly after! Without a word he grasped my arm and hurried me into a carriage, the door of which was standing open. "Here, cabby! Look sharp! We are rather late. Put on the steam, will you, and take us to the V— in time for the one o'clock train? You shall have a shilling extra."

"I'll do my very best." He drew up the windows on either side, tapped on the wood-work, and away we went as fast as the horse could go.

While we sat in the cavity of the good vessel, I would ask myself what o'clock it could be; I could hear the whistling of trains, now nearer and now farther off, punctuating the distance like the note of a bird in a forest. At any rate, we whirled into the station just as the great clocks were striking thirteen.

As we got on board I saw the motorman and conductor coming out of the station wine-shop. We sat down and opened the window. The sun made me sick with impatience and boredom as it let fall a golden stream, like an invitation to the feast at which I could not myself arrive before eight o'clock at night.

It was 1:30 p.m. when the train was climbing a rise and the sun was shining very brightly, and yet there was an exhilarating nip in the air, which set an edge to a man's energy: all over the countryside, suddenly, just at the stroke of a kind of half-humorous, half-surly half an hour, we were compassed round by a very thick fog, hoping that some change would take place in the atmosphere and weather. About two o'clock the mist cleared away, and we came through a village, then through a dark wood, then uphill, then downhill, till then the fog returned, and some of my comrades groaned. An unbearable heaviness weighed me down. Near three o'clock in the afternoon, this agonizing sensation affected me to an intense degree. Because of all that I didn't sleep a wink, and when I finally roused my friend Sherlock Holmes with all the will in the world at about 2:45, he did grudgingly get up and start sleepily organizing himself.

It must have been nearly three o'clock when we reached a narrow valley gouged between high, vertical walls. The terrain consisted mostly of thick slime mixed with petrified branches, but it changed little by little near four o'clock in the afternoon; it grew rockier and seemed to be strewn with pudding stones and a basaltic gravel called "tuff," together with bits of lava and sulfurous obsidian. The watch was a quarter-past four o'clock when we at last, after passing through the Valley, and over a river of little current, among tall stumps sheared off as if by giants, found ourselves at a town of sufficiently imposing proportions. And then it happened that the conductor shook my shoulder to warn me that we were at a transfer point. With the collar of his gray ulster turned up, he had a glass eye with the iris in the shape of a clock.

A lean, ferret-like man, furtive and sly-looking, was waiting for us upon the platform: "Only half past four! And here I am. At half past four!" Although he didn't have a watch and couldn't tell time too well, he was aware of passing time by the lengthening of the shadows. He said, "Doctor, won't you be very good to me and come with me. The next train won't be in for more than an hour."

I went and walked. Sherlock Holmes left me, but I had no time to be lonely, for within a half hour there arrived a torrential rain. The hurricane was unleashed at a speed of forty-five meters per second. Under these conditions houses topple, roof tiles puncture doors, iron railings snap in two, and twenty-four-pounder cannons relocate; no trains coming from the east. And so I trudged on through the muck and mire, through the deluge and a creaking and groaning of buildings and pipes, shafts and spires. Soon the whole village was electrified with the ghastly striking of some gigantic, buried clock. Boom . . . Boom . . . Boom . . . Then came the lightning, above, everywhere.

I reached the lodge at G— about five o'clock, drenched and haggard. Despite the tempest that raged above and around, it held its place and was very clean and neat: the ornamental windows were hung with little white curtains; the floor was spotless; the clock was hidden from sight by some envious shutters. Mrs. Kirke asked me if I wouldn't go down to the five o'clock dinner; and feeling a bit homesick, I thought I would.

In her topsy-turvy kitchen, I smelt the rich scent of the heating spices and admired the shining kitchen utensils, the polished clock decked in holly. The clock hands pointed to ten minutes after five.

I found Sherlock Holmes alone. A formidable array of bottles told me that he was to begin with reviving the drama.

"We can do nothing until seven o'clock tomorrow," he said, "now this storm has come on."

"Tomorrow it will all be over!" I cried hurriedly. "She'll be long gone."

"I sincerely hope so," said Sherlock Holmes curtly, and strode off.

I began to laugh weakly, the tears coming into my eyes. "Oh dear," I said, "let's send wires to everybody." But the lines were all jammed.

By six o'clock I ate supper, but I had no appetite. By seven o'clock, I was obliged to return to the drawing-room and lie down on the nearest sofa to recover. I sat and thought a doleful time: the clock struck eight, and nine, and still I was alone.

The time passed, slow, heavy, mysterious, stifling. Shortly before ten o'clock Mrs. Kirke called to me. It was when I stood before her, avoiding her eyes, that I took note of the surrounding objects in detail, and saw that her watch had stopped at twenty minutes to nine, and that a clock in the room had stopped at twenty minutes to nine. She saw, I suppose, the doubt in my face. The first stroke of the chime snapped me out of my musings.

"There is the ten o'clock bell ringing. In 1922 Warren G. Harding had ordered a whole salmon at ten o'clock in the evening, and a case of Coors beer. Do you not know that to-night, when the clock strikes midnight, all the evil things in the world will have full sway? Do you know where you are going, and what you are going to?" She was in such evident distress that I tried to comfort her, but without effect.

"Tell me," said she, with her arms composedly crossed, but with something in her dark cheek beating like a clock, "have you ever heard anyone whistle in the dead of the night?"

"Never," said I.

"You will. Laugh at me, I know, but every evening at lighting up o'clock sharp I have always heard a low, clear whistle . . ."

By this time it was about 10:30, and the long room was only dimly illuminated by the "dead lights" which are kept burning all night. At eleven o'clock she rose to leave me, but she paused at the door and looked back. The elegant little clock on the mantel-piece had struck "eleven with its silver sounds." The church steeples proclaimed eleven. She looked very strangely: "At twelve my horses turn into rats and I go off."

Though it is difficult to be exact in these matters, I took it that the very mystery of these words, as they dived down through the waves of a brain working, was in some way a counteractant to pass the time and for want of something better to do. I looked at my watch, and soliloquised on the length of the night: "Not quite midnight yet."

At about half past eleven she brought in a tray of tea and buttered scones and cakes. At exactly 11:32, I had blown out the candles. I was conscious of a mortal coldness and felt as if I should never again be warm.

Whenever the sound of the wind died away, the great agony came. I bethought myself to ring the bell just to relieve my feelings. But in about three minutes, I happened to look out of the window and the air was streaked with violent flashes of lightning. I couldn't stand this brightness, but it was then that the sound of a gong struck with violence: the church-clock had struck a quarter to twelve, and Sherlock Holmes had not come back yet.

It was nearly midnight . . . eleven forty-six before he entered, looking pale and worn. Behind Mrs. Kirke the new managers—M. Armand Moncharmin and M. Firmin Richard—came into the room. I saw a servant girl staring at the fire, saying little, and looking worried. As the clock excited, the time crept by with maddening slowness. The girl, who seemed to be looking with such anguished perplexity into the future, made the sign of the cross and began to pray.

At that moment, the clock on the mantlepiece gave its warning click and the first stroke of twelve struck.

The managers shuddered.

. . . two, three, four . . .

The perspiration streamed from their foreheads.

. . . five, six, seven . . .

The girl, showing every sign of unspeakable terror, counted the strokes. It suddenly seemed wrong to move again until the clock had stilled . . .

. . . eight . . . nine . . .

(?? Nine ??)

. . . ten . . . eleven . . .

Suddenly, the twelfth stroke sounded strangely in our ears.

When the clock stopped, the house was still as death, and nothing but the wailing of the wind broke the deep hush. Poor twelve o'clock scholars gave a sigh and rose from their chairs.

"I think we can go now," said Moncharmin.

"I think so," Richard agreed.

Then in a click of the clock, toot toot, and doff doff, suddenly a voice made them all turn round. A figure glided quietly from the little room behind the chimney-place of the big-crush room to the Rotunda. Another apparition—not a lovely one eskipping the clockback, crystal in carbon—appeared. I bowed to him. He gave me an almost imperceptible bow in return, without saying a word to me. Something clicked in his throat as if he had works in him like a clock, and was going to strike.

XV

BEING THE BALLAD OF WHAT CAME NEXT

They came through the hole in the night,
   And They sweet-talked it clear out of sight—
Figures, so strange, no GOD design'd
   To be a Part of Human-kind,

They slew my knight, to me sae dear;*
   They slew my knight, and drave his gear;
My servants a' for life did flee,
   And left us in extremitie.

Condemn'd by Fate, to wayward Curse,
   Of grudging foes, and empty Purse,
Plagues worse than fill'd Pandoras Box,
   I took my Leave of B——n Rocks,

Scarce had I left the evening Board
   And taking Horse, made Tracks toward
Jack's Castle when, giving Chase
   To flighty Deer, a horrid Face

---

* Holmes had gone as quickly as he had come.

Came into View: a demon'd Knight a' kernelling,
    Pursuing all infernal Things.
His Doublings and his Ternallings,
    His Forwardings and Sternallings.

The moan of the wind sunk silent and low,
    And the roaring torrent had ceased to flow;
The calm was more dreadful than raging storm,
    When the cold grey mist brought the ghastly Form!

This put me in a pannick Fright,
    Lest I should be devour'd quite. . .
A fiery Pulse beat in my Veins,
    From cold I felt resembling Pains.

So call me what you will, m' lads; riding on a Limb astride,
    Night and the Branches did me hide.
No one to love, none to Caress,
    Left all alone in this world's wilderness.

The Man and I commenc'd to quarrel:
    I to grumble, he to snarl.
The Man and I commenc'd to quarrel
    Anent the Style of our Apparel.

And, while Despair the scene was closing,
    'Mid storms of Fate opposing,
Distant winds began to wake,
    And roused the Genius of the Lake!

He 'gan to shake his foamy crest.
As the whirlwind nearer press'd
With a stern delight and strange,
I saw the spirit-stirring change,

And felt my heart more strongly bound,
Responsive to the lofty sound.
And so I turned my head; I fled
fantastic terrors. It resembled:

Through heather, mosse, 'mong frogs, and bogs, and fogs,
Hares, hinds, bucks, roes, men and dogs,
'Mongst craggy cliffs and thunder-batter'd hills,
I felt deep yearning and softly fills

Of light in the darkness, a shade between,
Creeping where no life is seen.
I mourn'd that demon'd scene no more
While joying in the mighty roar.

XVI

BEING MY BRIEF ASCENT INTO GOTHIC MYSTERY

A little further, the road wound into a deep valley. Mountains, whose shaggy steeps appeared to be inaccessible, almost surrounded it. Sometimes great masses of greyness, which here and there bestrewed the trees, produced a peculiarly weird and solemn effect, which carried on the thoughts and grim fancies engendered earlier, but I kept looking and ascending, with occasional periods of quick descent, but in the main always ascending.

After some time, the narrow path had opened suddenly onto a vista that exhibited the darkest horrors; perched atop a steep-rising hill was a vast castle with many turrets and towers. The ancient pile of stone seemed to stand the sovereign of the scene, and to frown defiance on all who dared to invade its solitary reign. Seven walls of stone formed an object so strong and old that it seemed to not have been builded but carven by giants out of the bones of the earth. Seven towers like daggers thrust into the belly of the sky, so high you can stand on the parapets and look down on the clouds.

I approached the Castle and saw everything: the immemorial masonry: the towers, the tracks. The shadows of time-eaten buttresses, of broken and lofty turrets. A wilderness of dark towers patched unevenly with black ivy and pointed blasphemously at heaven. It might enclose a whole world, it seemed, and its open gates yawned like a mouth before the drawbridge.

At once I exulted and feared, for now, for good or ill, the end was near. So as not to arouse any suspicion, I ventured to walk around it. As I went, the disorder of imagination was increased by the wildness of the surrounding scenery; by the gloomy Caverns and steep rocks, rising above each other; solitary clusters of Trees scattered here and there, among whose thick-twined branches the wind of night sighed hoarsely and mournfully; the shrill cry of mountain Eagles, who had built their nests among these lonely Desarts; the stunning roar of torrents, as swelled by rains as they rushed violently down tremendous precipices; and the dark waters of a silent sluggish stream which faintly reflected the moonbeams, and bathed the Rock's base on which I stood.

Suddenly, I found a sort of natural hollow in a rock, with an entrance like a doorway between two boulders. Looking at the view, I thought it was now time to end the scene, which was becoming too comically grave, so I went towards the door and touched it. The rusty hinges creaked, and it slowly opened.

XVII

BEING THE PAINTINGS THAT LINED THE HALLWAY ON THE OTHER SIDE OF THE DOOR

Suddenly there came into view a countenance (that of a decrepit old man, some sixty-five or seventy years of age)—a countenance which at once arrested and absorbed my whole attention, on account of the absolute idiosyncrasy of its expression. Any thing even remotely resembling that expression I had never seen before. I well remember that my first thought, upon beholding it, was that Retzch, had he viewed it, would have greatly preferred it to his own pictural incarnations of the fiend. As I endeavored, during the brief minute of my original survey, to form some analysis of the meaning conveyed, there arose confusedly and paradoxically within my mind the ideas of vast mental power, of caution, of penuriousness, of avarice, of coolness, of malice, of bloodthirstiness, of triumph, of merriment, of excessive terror, of intense—of supreme despair. I felt singularly aroused, startled, fascinated. "How wild a history," I said to myself, "is written within that bosom!" He was short in stature, very thin, and apparently very feeble. His clothes, generally, were filthy and ragged; but within the strong glare of a lamp, I perceived that his linen, although dirty, was of beautiful texture; and my vision deceived me, or, through a rent in a closely-buttoned and evidently second-handed roquelaire which enveloped him, I caught a glimpse both of a diamond and of a dagger.

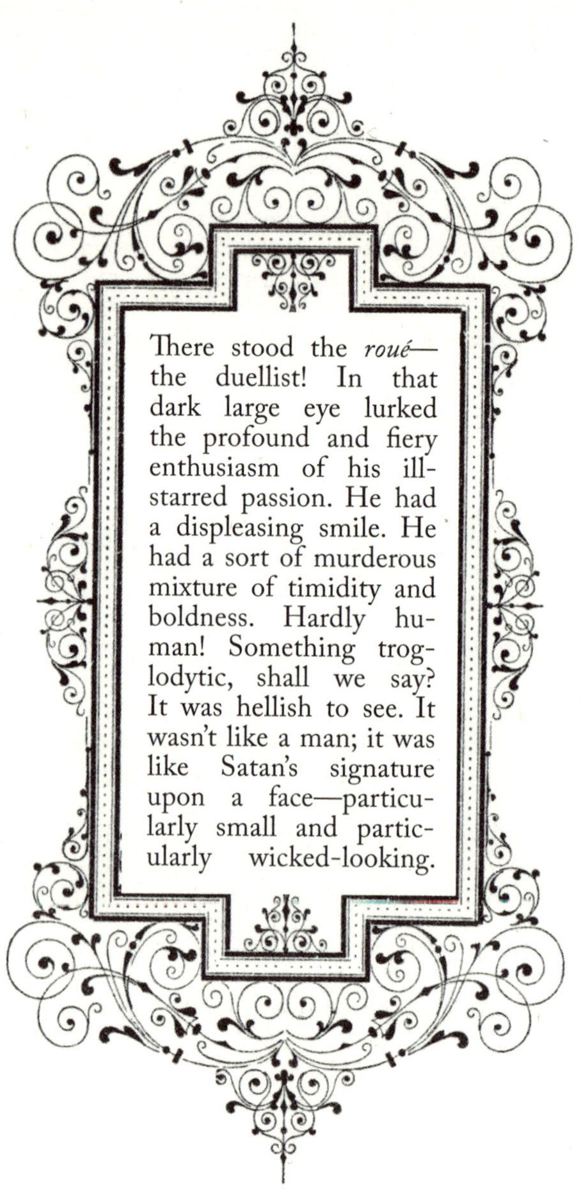

There stood the *roué*—the duellist! In that dark large eye lurked the profound and fiery enthusiasm of his ill-starred passion. He had a displeasing smile. He had a sort of murderous mixture of timidity and boldness. Hardly human! Something troglodytic, shall we say? It was hellish to see. It wasn't like a man; it was like Satan's signature upon a face—particularly small and particularly wicked-looking.

The small pen-and-ink sketch of the woman's head; it had evidently been drawn with great care, and by a true artist, for the woman's soul looked out of the eyes, and the lips were parted with a strange smile. The face; it brought to memory one summer evening, long ago; the long lovely valley, the river winding between the hills, the meadows and the cornfields, the dull red sun, and the cold white mist rising from the water. But the picture, the white-clad girl, the glance that came from those eyes, the smile on the full lips, or the expression of the whole face, it was a horrible sight. The most vivid presentment of evil I have ever seen.

A tall old man, clean shaven save for a long white moustache, and clad in black from head to foot, without a single speck of colour about him anywhere. His face was a strong—a very strong—aquiline, with high bridge of the thin nose and peculiarly arched nostrils; with lofty domed forehead, and hair growing scantily round the temples, but profusely elsewhere. His eyebrows were very massive, almost meeting over the nose, and with bushy hair that seemed to curl in its own profusion. The mouth, so far as I could see it under the heavy moustache, was fixed and rather cruel-looking, with peculiarly sharp white teeth; these protruded over the lips, whose remarkable ruddiness showed astonishing vitality in a man of his years. For the rest, his ears were pale and at the tops extremely pointed; the chin was broad and strong, and the cheeks firm though thin. The general effect was one of extraordinary pallor.

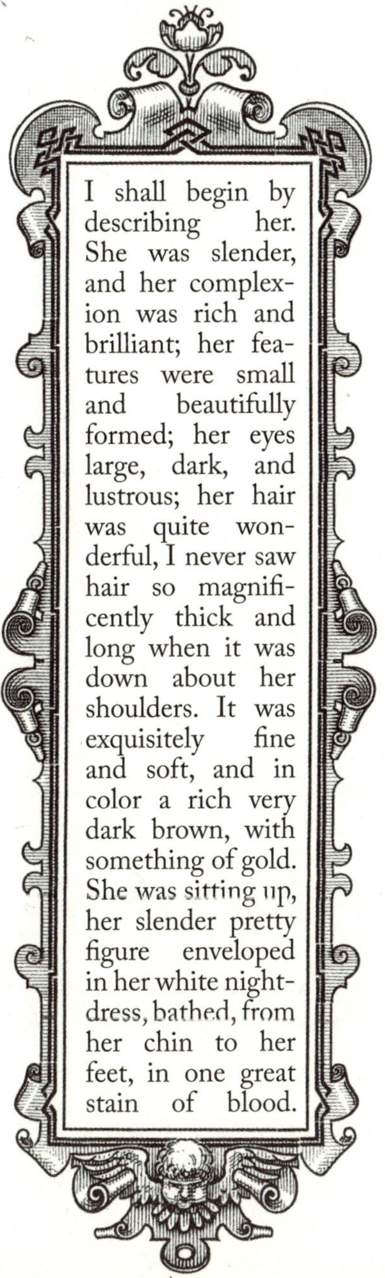

I shall begin by describing her. She was slender, and her complexion was rich and brilliant; her features were small and beautifully formed; her eyes large, dark, and lustrous; her hair was quite wonderful, I never saw hair so magnificently thick and long when it was down about her shoulders. It was exquisitely fine and soft, and in color a rich very dark brown, with something of gold. She was sitting up, her slender pretty figure enveloped in her white nightdress, bathed, from her chin to her feet, in one great stain of blood.

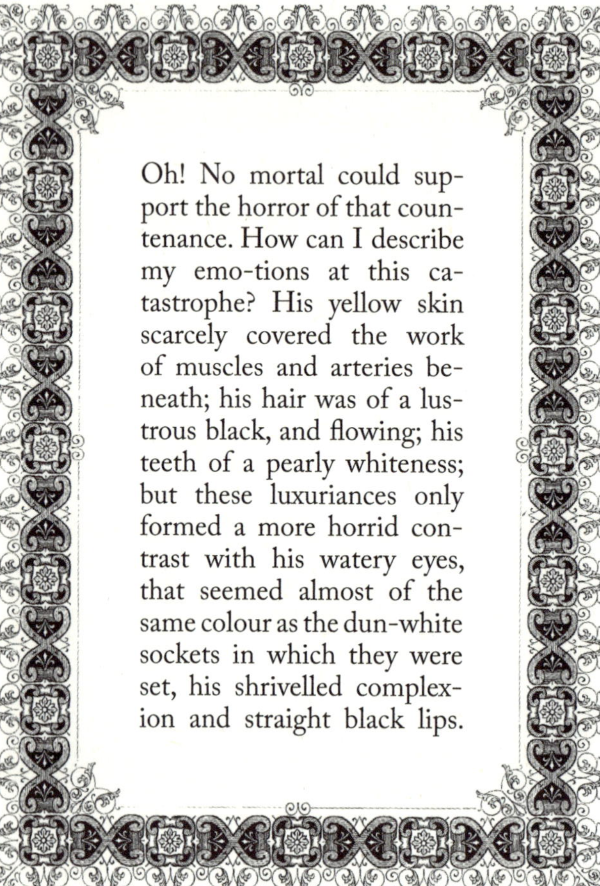

Oh! No mortal could support the horror of that countenance. How can I describe my emo-tions at this catastrophe? His yellow skin scarcely covered the work of muscles and arteries beneath; his hair was of a lustrous black, and flowing; his teeth of a pearly whiteness; but these luxuriances only formed a more horrid contrast with his watery eyes, that seemed almost of the same colour as the dun-white sockets in which they were set, his shrivelled complexion and straight black lips.

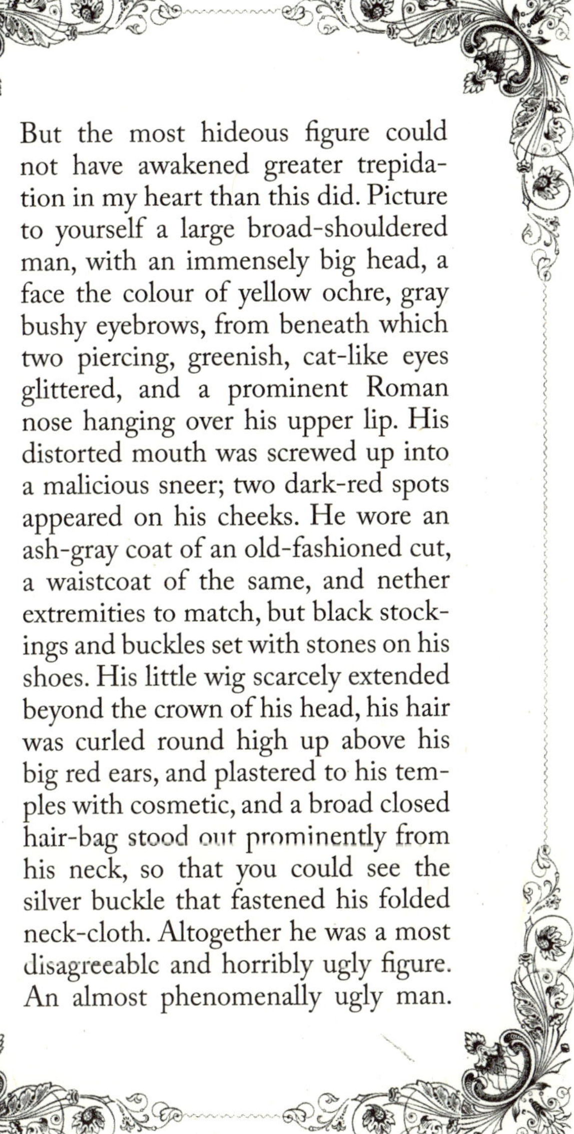

But the most hideous figure could not have awakened greater trepidation in my heart than this did. Picture to yourself a large broad-shouldered man, with an immensely big head, a face the colour of yellow ochre, gray bushy eyebrows, from beneath which two piercing, greenish, cat-like eyes glittered, and a prominent Roman nose hanging over his upper lip. His distorted mouth was screwed up into a malicious sneer; two dark-red spots appeared on his cheeks. He wore an ash-gray coat of an old-fashioned cut, a waistcoat of the same, and nether extremities to match, but black stockings and buckles set with stones on his shoes. His little wig scarcely extended beyond the crown of his head, his hair was curled round high up above his big red ears, and plastered to his temples with cosmetic, and a broad closed hair-bag stood out prominently from his neck, so that you could see the silver buckle that fastened his folded neck-cloth. Altogether he was a most disagreeable and horribly ugly figure. An almost phenomenally ugly man.

XVIII

BEING MY DECOROUS DESCENT INTO THE DEPTHS OF GOTHIC TERROR

In the next room, the air was awfully stuffy. It was startlingly like the image conveyed to me in Dr. Seward's diary of the opening of Miss Westenra's tomb: a lofty chamber, hung round with dark arras, and so spacious, that the lamp did not shew its extent. It was, however, light enough for our purposes, with its red hangings, its chairs, its carpet covered in red velvet. After feeling the carpet in the most serious manner possible, I rose hastily from my knees, standing up before a black velvet chair and ample crimson curtains of rather expensive material and modern make. Beneath, were tables, with fruit, wine, Cherry Brandy, and olives stretched along, till their various colours melted in the distance into damask roses.

On a table by the dark verdure, a profusion of viands were spread; amongst others were sweetbreads stewed in saffron soups and lamb, a chicken done up some way with red pepper, which was very good but thirsty. In the best chair, the faded red cover of a thin old-fashioned gilt-edged album—*An Ode to the Box,* by Roderick Sackbut—lay. A mandolin and an apple lay down at the feet of the chair, which I imagined Catherine had left, in a warmer situation.

I shuddered as I bent over to touch the chair, straining over the table with bowed head, and humped back. I felt a chillness creep all round my heart, my knees tottered, and, meanwhile, I had opened this book. It, of course, abounded with allusions to the snuff box, from the red cover at the beginning to the red cover at the end. I never was happier in my life, and

I believe it was the universal feeling among the cups and the dusky curtains. A goodly sight! O! I was ready to leap through the rusty old bars for joy!—O! I could have kissed the very horse that brought me here, fainting and half chloroformed. I could have clasped the red walls to my bosom as a garment of eternal peace.

This enthusiastic soliloquy was interrupted by a rustling noise . . . on which I turned the light of my lantern. I fancied I saw a man's face within the dusky curtains, and for a brief period, I once more relapsed into insensibility, which made my blood run cold. What it was, whether man or beast, I could not tell; I did not wait to catch another glance, but flew from the room by a door which opened to a dark, tunnel-like passage, through which came a deathly, sickly odour, the odour of old earth newly turned.

As I went through the passage the smell grew closer and heavier. It was quite dark, but for a faint red glimmer at a distant corner of the wall. Down the crimson'd dungeon, emblems of Death were seen on every side: skulls, shoulder-blades, thigh-bones, and other leavings of Mortality being only lit by loopholes in the heavy masonry. Now and then fantastic shadows were silhouetted against the stones.

Around a corner of the tomb, it was then very dark; the perspective one way only a crooked prolongation of this great dungeon; the shorter perspective in the other direction terminating in a gloomy red light, and the gloomier entrance to a black tunnel. That dark passage was entirely gothic, and the scattered lamps made the darkness greater when outside their individual radius, until now when a new light flared out, led the eye, to a thin veil of carnation: through the dark, at the further end, a flight of stairs mounted to a door covered with red baize.

I went for the stairs. A little closer—put your heart in your ears—I heard suppressed sighs and gentle movements going on through the door, and in a moment I perceived a rusty iron door, half overgrown with creeping plants, but with smoke issuing from its crevices.

At first I thought I was in a dream as I went up the steps—then I had a vague memory of something long and dark with red eyes—but like all things human it came to an end, and I reached the door, prepared to quit the dungeon.

. . . And then . . . And then I heard voices and footsteps on the stairs. I heard them coming upstairs, and I had just time to slip into a closet and draw the door to (for I am a trap-door lover and I open and shut what I please and as I please); it was not quite closed, but nearly so.

In a minute the gentleman reached the spot before the doorway, knocked at the red baize door, and it was opened by his friend. Then I thought something must be strangely the matter with me, and directly I dropt down to hear more.

"There is nothing to be got by the rest," said one of his companions, without any further explanation, and disappeared.

I listened with apparently great attention; as the reader knows, I was already an adept in the art of the castle. I listened attentively, and could hear a deep half-suppressed sigh, and then footsteps, and the Countess, immediately—horror of horrors—she after this came straight to the closet and gave a slight scream on discovering me there. I blushed up to the ears, and tried to stammer out an excuse. She stared at me at first in silent amasement; but at last said—

"How came you here, sir, tell me?"

"I was here when you came up, and when I heard you coming, I hid myself, I don't know why."

For some minutes she seemed to consider and examine me attentively. She then said—

"Can you be discreet?"

"Oh, yes, ma'am."

"You will never tell any one what you have seen?"

"No ma'am."

She took my hand in hers, and I beheld a countenance of angelic beauty and expression. Her hair of a shining raven black, and curiously braided; her eyes were dark, but gentle, although animated; her features of a regular proportion, and her complexion wondrously fair, each cheek tinged with a lovely pink.

When the knock came, I took my courage à deux mains and entered it; and the Countess immediately followed my example, stepped to the door and opened it.

It was a voluptuous scene, that masquerade. But first let me tell of the room into which M. le Vicomte de Chagny and I had dropped. The room, at one and the same time, an exact copy of the torture-chamber of the rosy hours of Mazenderan, the whole discreetly lighted by a shaded lamp standing on a small round table: the wooden bedstead, the waxed mahogany chairs, the chest of drawers, those brasses, the little square antimacassars carefully placed on the backs of the chairs, the clock on the mantelpiece and the harmless-looking ebony caskets at either end, lastly, the whatnot filled with shells, with red pin-cushions.

I had hardly begun my titillations on both the room and its reasonable furniture, when I looked towards the bed again; my bodily eye was cheated into the convulsive throbs of their whole bodies. All about the room, nothing was heard but slaps on bottoms, and the wildest rollicking laughter—a mutual slapping of arses and seizing of pricks and cunts, a very exciting game, which soon brought evidences of renewed vigour in all the room.

Not one minute had been gone when there came a gentle knock at the door; Isabella had arrived. Hardly two minutes would elapse before we would hear the Portuguese and the French for "cunt." Various allusions of that sort were heard. The heart-quaking sound *of Consul Romanus.* Remote voices. And, soon after, we would hear broken and unintelligible phrases; then strong ejaculations.

XIX

BEING THE CLIMAX OF THIS NOVEL

"Oh, Jem!" Jane ejaculated.

"Ah!" ejaculated Grace.

"Humph!" ejaculated Mrs. Thorne.

"Humph!" ejaculated Chet's mother.

"Dolly!" ejaculated Mrs. Boncassen. "She's a woman, through and through, if ever thar was one."

"She is," ejaculated Keith, looking meditatively at the stove.

"Very glad, very glad!" she ejaculated.

"Good lord!" ejaculated the old man, sitting down feebly and staring.

"Brian!" ejaculated the banker. (The clerk ejaculated the length of his toothpick.)

"Me?" ejaculated the Society Editor, disdainfully.

"As sure as I'm in this room!" he ejaculated.

"But—me!" ejaculated Victor, rolling his eyes upwards in astonishment.

"Confusion!" ejaculated Piers.

"It was a confession," I ejaculated.

"Heaven give me patience!" ejaculated Penrose.

"Never!" ejaculated Hippy fervently.

"Never!" ejaculated Pendry and Mail together, Tonkin smoking in silence.

Phillip gasped and stared in amazement. "Dondersteen!" he ejaculated loudly, and nearly dropped his half-conscious and swaying burden on the ground.

“What’s that?” ejaculated Joseph Stagg in a sharp tone.

“A comet of gold!” ejaculated the captain. “Thatsh good!”

Freddie nearly rolled out of his chair.

The father of Samoylov threw himself back, and ejaculated broken words behind his wife’s ear. The mother ejaculated in a sudden burst of excitement; she minded less his somewhat rude ejaculation: “Ho! Ho! South! South! The vervloekte Keerl! the plepshurk! the smeerlap!”

“What on earth does this mean?” I ejaculated.

“Can’t you see with your own eyes?” he ejaculated, attempting to walk on.

“Ha!” ejaculated the old lady.

“Hum!” ejaculated Mr. Stagg.

“O Lord!” ejaculated Titmouse, involuntarily, and almost unconsciously, staring stupidly at Gammon. Mr. Gammon soon *felt* the presence of his secret.

“Lord, Mr. Gammon!” ejaculated Titmouse, passing his hand hastily over his damp forehead—his agitation visibly increasing. Gammon gazed at him for a moment with fury; and “Good thunder!” they ejaculated.

Dinmont at length got up, and, having shaken his huge dreadnought greatcoat, as a Newfoundland dog does his shaggy hide when he comes out of the water, ejaculated. The Little Russian ejaculated. Aunt Nettie, of course, ejaculated, “Goodness gracious!” and laughed.

Ben Zoof broke out into the most vehement ejaculations.

“Gentle!” ejaculated Bartlemy, the artist, with profound conviction.

“He’s our little pet,” said Rob. “Come here, Ben, dear. Ben Zoof!” he called aloud.

“Ben who?” inquired the major.

“Zoof! Ben Zoof!” ejaculated Servadac, who could scarcely shout loud enough to relieve his pent-up feelings. “That’s our—our nice—gentle—oh, dear me!—our nice, gentle, old Ben.”

“Well, this is a pretty piece of business!” ejaculated Marilla.

“Incredible!” ejaculated the colonel.

"Incredible!" echoed the major. But of a sudden he ejaculated "God bless my soul!" and collapsed onto a settee as if his legs had been mown from under him. "Holy cats!" he ejaculated.

"Brother!" ejaculated the other.

"Bless my soul!" ejaculated the landlord, in bewilderment. "Where did he come from?"

"Bless me! Yes!" ejaculated the hardware man finally.

"Humph!" ejaculated the hardware dealer again.

"Eh wow! Eh wow!" ejaculated the honest farmer, as he looked round upon his friend's miserable apartment and wretched accommodation—"What's this o't! what's this o't!" he ejaculated.*

The place was, in fact, becoming less tenable. Members of the congregation were interjecting, "Glory Hallelujah!" "Praise be His Name!" and the other worshipful ejaculations which make a sort of running accompaniment on such occasions.

"Great Heavens above!" ejaculated Piers.

"Heaven be praised!" ejaculated the captain, and he went on in the tones of a keen excitement.

The Dominie groaned deeply, and ejaculated.

At this unexpected and involuntary explosion of his weapon, the Dominie exclaimed, "Prodigious!" which is his usual ejaculation when astonished. "Great God!" ejaculated the others, but "Pro-di-gi-ous!" was

---

* He would slip down into the basement and ejaculate, pausing in his restless walk and looking somewhat dazed on his friend, as if he were just waking from a feverish sleep. He came, now, directly to the underground parlour, hat on head and ebony stick in hand.

"Dondersteen!" he ejaculated again.

"What is it now, Jakob?" queried a woman's voice peremptorily.

"Dondersteen!" he shouted in his turn, swearing lustily.

"Did ever anyone hear the like!" ejaculated Marilla, who had listened in dumb amazement.

"Pitcher of George Washington!" ejaculated the man.

"Pitcher of George—" The rest of his favourite ejaculation was smothered by the press of other emotions. He looked round the room—now almost deserted—somewhat at a loss for words.

the only ejaculation they ever extorted from the much-enduring man. This escaped my notice at the time, you may easily believe; but in talking over the scene afterwards, Hazlewood made us very merry with the Dominie's ignorant but zealous valor.

The good Dominie uttered his usual ejaculation of "Prodigious!" and then strode back to his post.

Hazlewood seconded him with great spirit. "Oh, your Excellency," ejaculated the orderly, "look there! look there!" Then pointed to a table, upon which was some cold meat, and a spirit lamp, and a captain of the 8th Artillery and two officers who had presumed to do their duty.

Hazlewood longed to accompany the military. The Dominie looked upon him with that sort of surprise with which we can conceive a tame bear might regard his future associate, the monkey, on their being first introduced to each other. Sir Robert Hazlewood was rather puzzled at this intimation. "Please!" he ejaculated.

But the other heeded not, and with head thrown back against the wall, and brawny chest expanded, almost drowned the rest of the voices by his marvellous roars. Then with an ejaculation of "Here goes!" he jumped over the intervening crack of space and landed in the middle of us like a sack of coal. Had I not been seated really I think he would have knocked me off the rock.

"Cursed friar!" I ejaculated mentally.

"Well, I never!" ejaculated Abner Balberry.

"For Heaven's sake!" ejaculated Aunt Nettie. "Thanks to the saints no further harm was done." And with this compassionate ejaculation, she retreated into her own premises. No wonder the girls ejaculated at her smartness.

The good Dominie stretched out with a murmur of relief and comfort. The ground felt like the softest couch. "Hullo!" he ejaculated softly.

"You!" ejaculated Halicarnassus, contemptuously.

"The devil!" ejaculated Pritchen.

As for the Dominie, my father (my father??) took an opportunity of begging to exchange snuff boxes (snuff boxes!!) with him. The honest gentleman was much flattered with the proposal, extolled the beauty of his snuff box excessively, smiled at the snuff box fondly, caressing it with his finger.

My father looked at him again. "This snuff box, to which so great a value is attached! How did you get such a . . . Gold!" he ejaculated, but the Dominie made no answer.

Peter meanwhile was looking at the snuff box, which the priest still held in his hand, and admiring its brave repoussé work of leaves and flowers, and the escutcheon engraved on the lid. "My that's fine!" he ejaculated, wiping the perspiration from his forehead with the sleeve of his coat.

The Dominie groaned. "Wait. I'll tell you the whole story. You shall see for yourself."

"Go on," ejaculated Tregear.

"Yes, yes, yes," cried Tinfoil, "where did you get such a thing as this?"

"Oh!" I cried.

The Duchess's eyes were intent. "The story—? Tell me the story," she pronounced in a breath, with imperious eagerness.

He told his story accordingly, often interrupted by ejaculations.

XX

BEING THE TATTERED TESTIMONY OF HOW THE DOMINIE OBTAINED THE COVETED SNUFF BOX

In the second week of October, 18—, in the country near D——, something strange had happened.

Seven months previous, a warm whim, a wanton toy had just taken me, and I had spent a whole summer and autumn in travelling: coming from Knightbr——, sir, I set off for ————, going to ——'s in the —— Isles, where Martha G— resided in the favourite center of sense (in a certain little church not far from ——— Street). My aunt was there (her Catalonian father was a merchant residing in the —— Isles) and my four lovers, though they had said, one and all, they would not come.

About a month after our first intercourse in the —— Isles, the next Thursday I went down to ——shire to see either the heroic captive or Madame de S—, and very soon returned to D——.

D—— was glowingly alive all over, and tossing with burning impatience for the renewal of joys that had sinned on a summer's day. People came from a distance of ten leagues around to S— Place, which had been in D—— about three months. Julia and Georgiana G——, daughters of an English baronet, Mdlle. Mathilde de ——, heiress of a Belgian count, and sundry other children of patrician race passed through D——. But, at any rate, after a day or two of residence in D——, all the stories and subjects of conversation which engross petty towns and petty people at the outset had fallen into profound oblivion; the fool of a fellow came to me with messages.

Sir W—— H——'s coach arrived at D—— about three o'clock in the morning. (This Sir W—— was a gentleman who lived about three miles out of town, in ——shire, I believe.)

Setting foot outside, I began my discovery with a snarl: "What in the d——l's name do you want?"

At once, Sir W—— said, indicating an old man with a profusion of silver-gray curly hair, "Old V____ came with a message from his master, Mr. H. . . ." And old V____ consequently stood trembling and pale, waiting.

As I stood staring, the man-servant appeared to meditate for an instant, the lines about his mouth becoming very marked indeed.

"D—n it, man, end the frolic at once," I said. "I am feverish."

Old V____ jumped up and immediately read:

> My dear ——,
>
> Visit immediately the town of X——. Mr. H . . . ., so experienced, so learned, expects you, and will join you at once. Proceed without delay to X—— and report to one Mr. ——. He has lost a snuff box, which you must recover as quickly as possible. Be on the look-out, for you know neither the day nor hour when your —— (I don't wish to blaspheme, so I'll leave a blank) cometh.
>
> Yours truly,
> Mr. H . . . .

Soon this Sir W—— and old V____ left the clean streets where there were dwelling-houses, and I was left to admire the stars of night.

Our friend B___d had been there with eyes to see and heart to feel. He turned to give me a smile before he helped me back into the outer room.

B___d, by the bye, was called the Hermit of ——— Street, and of his birth and connections little was known. He stayed with me that evening, and spoke in whispers, and the ordinary business was transacted with celerity and quietness.

"Mors communis omnibus!" whispered B___d, and when he had finished whispering these words in my ear, *——any other man would have sunk down to the centre——but I was prepared to meet all objections, and during the interval of silence, I replied, "——."*

"And that," said he.

"D——d nonsense . . . . ," said I—and so my remarks which had been in circulation about him continued, with ghastly vivacity. "After coming to the very door! What a peculiar proceeding! His gold *snuff box,* his fine *periwig.* D—n my creditors!"

Our friend B___d looked as if he did not understand. Turning to me he said bluntly— "You will seek out lodgings in X——."

Quitting the window, I walked back to the hearth, the strokes of the clock striking in my head——

"Of course I shall seek out lodgings in X——," I answered.

After two days' travelling (railroads were not then in existence) I arrived, one wet October afternoon, in the town of X——. The autumn sun, rising over the ——shire hills, disclosed a pleasant country; woods brown and mellow varied the fields from which the harvest had been lately carried. At a distance of five miles, a valley, opening between the low hills, held in its cups the great town of X——.

X—— was all stir and bustle when we entered it. Sir Thomas ——'s eldest daughter was just setting off on a visit to the Duchess of D_____;

* EDITOR'S COMMENTARY: Another edition of this book has the word "Merde!" in lieu of the —— above.

the Duchess of B—— was with Sir William ——'s lady. A crowd in the ——— Street seemed to be on a strain of mingled emotions.

Towards the K—— bridge, a fiacre conveyed me to the Hotel de ——, where I had been advised by a fellow-traveller to put up.

I came in without knocking and, as I passed by the ordinary sitting-room, Madame de S— was resting angularly on the sofa. She told me Mr. H . . . . was above.

Upstairs on the landing, the first sight that struck me was Mr. H . . . . pulling and hauling this coarse country stammel towards a couch. The Bishop of D—— was on the landing and had come to suggest to his young friend a stroll.

Mr. H . . . . looked a little silly and sat down on a chair whilst we stood like criminals under examination. I said I was sent to know how Mr. —— did.

"And your name is——?"

"My name is ——; I live in such a street"—naming the street—"at the sign of the Cradle in D——."

Mr. H . . . ., on hearing what I said, hung his head a little; but instantly recovering himself, he said to me: "Where in the name of h——ll is the snuff box of Mr. ——?"

I said: "Dr. B—— had not done it. Perhaps the next coachman might have done it. Don't be afraid. I'll follow the other, by G——, to . . . . if I have to."

Mr. H . . . . continued: "And what the d——l am I going to do in the meanwhile?"

We looked at each other. Then ideas began to come. "Has Mr. —— gone out that way?" said I.

"No, sir. No one has come out this way."

Just then I turned my face a little to the light; the approach of twilight and my position in the window gave me a full view of a fine-featured, shapely, healthy country lad with a genuine —shire countenance. As I moved—stopp'd—watched from the window, he tapped his snuff box and took a pinch of snuff. Then swiftly, stealthily, almost with the air of a man committing felony, he slipped his snuff box under his left arm.

"D___ me, he may bolt with the box!"

I left the building and returned to —— Street.

When I entered the little town street, it was a fine night, and the streets were dry and even clean for X——; there was a crescent curve of moonlight to be seen by the parish church tower, and a chill frost-mist was rising from the river on which X—— stands; there was no one to be seen. He was gone.

My emotions were indescribable. I felt the usual consequence of the first launch into vice, sampled XXXX whiskey 'till I could hardly see, an' dallied with th' —th regiment, Commodore J——, and Major — de Coverley at my lodgings.

When Major — de Coverley stepped into the hall with his fierce and austere dignity, turning to me he began abruptly: "How well you like X——!"

"To h——ll with your X——," said I.

He pull'd out a cambric handkerchief—gave a low sigh—but held his peace. "Cannot you manage, my dear, for a single time, to **** *** ** *** ****** ?"

"No, no," said I, shaking my head sideways—"'tis dirt, the whole scene. Joltheads, nincompoops, sh—t-a-beds!" I permitted myself to laugh with a degree of scorn I took no pains to temper or hide.

His fury boiled up, and when he had sworn half-a-dozen vulgar oaths, without, however, venturing to lift the whip, Major — de Coverley demanded at last: "Spiritualize! You must lug out for the damage you have done—you're a trespasser."

" . . . .," said I. "I'll not stay a day longer in X—— than I'm obliged."

Mr. H . . . . stole in upon us, before either of us was aware. "What have you been saying all over X——?"

"About?" said I.

"De omnibus rebus," replied he, "truly you are not as fine a fellow as your plebeian brother by a long chalk."

I really intended to leave X—— the next morning.

From the first week of my residence in X—— I felt my occupation irksome. The thing itself—this fuss over a trifling thing like a snuff box—was a dry and tedious task enough, but had that been all, I should long have borne with the nuisance.

After the awful evening when I stood by, a watchful but ignored spectator of a lost snuff box, it seemed the Hotel de —— was very far from resembling heaven ("Is he in h——ll?" you might say): the isolated clinks and thumps of Major — de Coverley's horseshoes falling to the ground outside the window; the cry of profound satisfaction of young ——shire heiresses doing it to Lord . . . . At meals, Madame de S— extended a claw-like hand, glittering with costly rings, towards the paper of cakes, took up one and devoured it, displaying her big false teeth ghoulishly.

As to Mr. H . . . ., he was so much my superior in every sense, that I felt it too much to the disadvantage of the gratitude I owed him. His very particular friend, Mr. ——, had more than once assessed—but it is as fallacious as the breath of fame—that I had beaten about for many hours and had been obliged to return nearly to the same spot from which I had departed.

"What in the d——l's name do you want me to do?" I asked, having lost the scent.

"I wish you could see yourself. D—n it, man, let the poor fellow have back his snuff box!" he replied.

Trembling and dreading the issue, I should have made a conscience to die in his debt. But Mr. H . . . ., who penetrated my uneasiness, did not suffer me to languish under it, and acquainted me, that having taken a solid sincere affection to me, he would dispatch a man "to see a sick lady who has sent for me," he said like a fish out of water.

"What sick lady?—where does she live?"

"In —shire."

"—shire? That is a hundred miles off!"

The day he returned, the man-servant appeared and seated himself on a low stool close to the fire. After a great many arguments used to comfort and reconcile me to my fate, he told me:

> Madame la Duchesse de —— knew you from the description of a solicitor of — Street, she told me, speaking positively. After some critical remarks upon the personalities of the ——regiment of infantry, she spoke of the snuff box, but— she stopped suddenly, and began accordingly to interest herself a little about the horse which he, Mr. H . . . ., might probably have been the sole master of at the B—— races . . . She tried to make her tone insouciant, but she was conscious of her cheeks getting hot. Mr. H . . . . perhaps brought on this change.

Mr. H . . . ., on hearing what the man-servant said, hung his head a little. The man-servant carried on:

> Madame la Duchesse de —— continued in a changed tone and glancing towards the staircase she said, with unexpected insight in the further development of the affair of the snuff box; as though there were some predestination, some indication in it . . . .

. . . .

. . . . "There's Major ——. He was an eminent pickpocket; there's Justice Ba——r, was a shoplifter, and both of them were burnt in the hand; and then——"

"And then?" I asked.

He looked a little angrily at first. "I wish you could see, d——it! When one has the means of doing something of the sort, it seems, full well I wot, they will abuse it! A valuable article, a small snuff box, to be exact—has been stolen by one of these 'delicate' gentlemen!"

"Yes, yes, sh—sh—sh—" I ejaculated impolitely.

Mr. H . . . . soon followed with a hollow, dry, excoriating laugh: "Major — de Coverley! 'Major —' is *that Major — de Coverley!*"

"Zounds!——————————————————————— Z——ds!" cried I.

There was no exit possible from this profound knowledge. In all the modes, from the first week of my residence in X—— to my new lodgings at a brush-maker's in E—— street, I had an unpleasant mental vision of Major — de Coverley, but I did not know he was master of all the plots and conspiracies to do with the matter of this snuff box!

"Where in the name of hell is that Major — de Coverley?" Mr. H . . . . continued.

"——'s!" said I.

The valet de place put on his hat, and led the way—and it was therefore to the house on —— Street we were driven.

On the way there were dwelling-houses and shops, churches, and public buildings; we left all these, and turned down to the ——sky Bridge, stopped in the middle of —— Street.

When we entered *** at twelve-thirty, a crowd in the —— Street house (the ——regiment of infantry) was waiting in the anteroom. Major — de Coverley paused in the doorway with a frown of puzzled disapproval. Mr. H . . . ., who had watched, perhaps brought on this change.

With repressed glee, I gave Major — de Coverley an oath to sign, his admission of guilt.

"Well, old fellow, d___ me, if you ain't a trump," Major — de Coverley observed.

"His snuff box?" I asked.

"I wish you could see yourself," Major — de Coverley retorted.

And we lapsed into strained debate. Major — de Coverley, a Spartan in adversity, did not flinch once throughout the whole hideous ordeal, had felt secure of victory, until the appearance of the Duke of ——. After the Duke of ——, followed by a very plain Commodore J——, then a certain Prince S—— arrived in the —— Street house, Major — de Coverley straightened with astonishment. At first he hesitated, but when we had lit our cigars he said—

"Lord ——; in the name of the Father, the Son, and——"

There was a fearful scream, which almost froze our hearts to hear. He started forward in a straight line, and the wall of officers before him parted like the Red Sea.

Major — de Coverley ran off. Most of the servants fled. Weary as I was of the atmosphere of brutality and insolence in which I had constantly lived at X——, I had no inclination now on casting anchor in calmer regions, and I ran, singing, after him.

I desired him, then, to pave the way for the accomplishment of my scheme, the object of which was to recover a lost snuff box to Mr. ——!

* * *

After my vainly attempting to stop him, I abandoned myself entirely to a heavy loss. He shook me off, though he seemed greatly moved by my tears, and ran in the direction of the ——y Bridge.

Mr. H . . . ., after bidding me take care of myself, and recommending me to my repose, left me to myself. I went to bed, and felt immediately a heat, a fire run like a hue-and-cry through every part of my body; I burnt, I glowed.

Next morning I awoke from prolonged and sound repose with the impression that I was yet in X——, and perceiving it to be broad daylight I started up, imagining that I had overslept myself.

A bell suddenly rang out, its sound intensified by the stillness until the owner of the box, Mr. ——, stood at a little distance, reluctantly, at the door of the debtors' prison!

"Vell! vell! my dear," quoth Mr. ——.

"Lord! Mr. ——, what must I do? Major — de Coverley had kidnaped the snuff box . . . . . . and . . . . . ."

That Mr. —— in a clear, full-bodied voice that was gruff with age and resonant with ancient eminence and authority, said: "A tragic event occurred at D—— last night, or rather this morning. A man was condemned to death for the box and its contents.

"After making a careful examination of the little world of D——, a former member of the Convention (his name was G——), mentioned with a sort of horror that he had mistaken my snuff box for another's! The wrong man! Quite dead, and had apparently been so for an hour or two . . . *D—n!* Did you ever see such a mess? That old wretch of a G—— . . ."

"Mr. ——, what must I do?" I replied.

"I'll—I'll discharge your debt—if you will leave the house, leave X——; the remembrance of what we have done wrapt up in an eternal silence, as if it had never happened. You shall always have my respect, and——" and there he stopped.

"Is anything wrong, gentlemen?" Mr. H . . . . opened my room door softly, and came in.

"Where's ——?" said I, naming our host awkwardly enough, and whispering to myself: "Pray, my dear, do not be startled . . . "

Delighted as I was with the confused plan in my head, I was easily alarmed, to the habits and purposes of Mr. H . . . .'s nicety, and I seized my hat, and forced my reluctant body out of the new lodgings and returned to —— Street.

Unconsciously I steered my course towards the country. A chill frost-mist was rising from the river on which X—— stands and along whose banks the road which intersected the plain passed.

A few paces out of X——, I quitted the wall and once more turned my face towards X——.

"Queer place—strange thing—serves me right—very," I thought at once.

But at the same time Lord F____, a dandy sportsman and the butt of the regulars of X——, rode one horse, which he had run at the B—— races. "Have you seen the hounds this way?" demanded Lord F____.

"Hounds!"

"Dogs, I mean," continued Lord F____, a sheet of paper in one hand and his watch in the other.

I looked round the fields from which the harvest had been lately carried; nothing.

"They've got off clean," I said. "No." . . . And just then one of the little demons appeared. We looked at each other. Then a glow, a softness, that seemed—that seemed . . . a dull metallic yellow . . . appeared to me in that light . . .

I was instantly borne away down along the banks of the river, the water, so—deep and abundant. I stood awhile, leaning over a wall; and looking down at the current, I watched a thin shining object that had done me harm: the two words . . . . . . and . . . . . . : the snuff box of Mr. ——!

XXI

BEING MY FATEFUL FIGHT FOR THE SNUFF BOX

My father interrupted the theologian at this point and, turning to me, said, "My son, if you had been in X—— the next morning, you could have restored me to happiness and virtue!"

"Chances are it's another counterfeit," I thought. The fine gold glowed and burned like a lamp, but it had little effect.

I suddenly felt the pressure of despair. It was such a slender hope, so frail and so dangerous to think that less than a fortnight ago, less than one little brief fortnight ago, I had never heard of the horrible snuff box, which had already caused so much anxiety and trouble.

Just then one of the little demons that inhabit a chair in this room got up, and shuffled rather than walked toward us at ever increasing speed. I soon realized he was deliberately affronting my ears and eyes with his own peculiar gesture of weariness and his way of talking. I had it in my heart to hate him—no, not hate, revulsion. It was natural. Who the man was, or what he was, I didn't care a dump.

"His name is Prince Paradox," said Dorian. "Years ago he was christened Prince Charming."

"I recognize him in a flash!" exclaimed the duchess.

The others drew back a respectful distance as the prince placed a heavy purse in the priest's hands and said, in a low voice:

"I'd like to speak with God."

With eager hands he took the box, and going to the light, bent over it. For a moment the Prince paused, following footsteps. As he saw the pearls, the cross, his face, ghastly pale, turned toward the ceiling. His brow contracted in a frown, and he crushed the box in his hand. "Was this some absurd joke? It's a fake," he said hoarsely.

The Dominie groaned. He looked utterly shocked and started to melt. The crowd went wild!

Above all its noise a voice suddenly came to me.

A voice of singular charm and grace.

The sound of wind in leaves.

Of leaves and flowers.

"Impossible," I thought. "It couldn't be."

I stared in amazement, and at last turned to Catherine's side with a look of exultation.

And there she was. Dressed in white, as always—a frock of I know not what supple fabric, that looked as if you might have passed it through your ring, and fell in multitudes of small soft creases. Two big red roses drooped from her bodice.

I stared at her and she stared back. Her eyes were as hard as the bricks in my front walk. I shrugged the stare off and said: "I've been looking all over for you."

"I have something to tell you," she whispered in my ear.

And just then the Prince came up to her.

"Beautiful Fawn," said he.

She hesitated, looking at her lover—but, surely, it was obvious—pitifully. So sadly, so pitifully, that it caused the tears to surge as readily as the Fountain of all the Sorrows inside me. A dull pain began to shoot insistently through my body and engulfed it like a charge of electricity. For a moment I was conscious of nothing else. Then, as the couple passed by, Lady Catherine turned and looked upon me. She pointed to a bergère, the table or the mantel. She seemed beside herself with anxiety. She went with the prince, of course, to the next room, where a splendid throne had been erected. A beautiful crown of flowers was placed on her head.

"I wish I could bear this dreadful pain," I thought. "What do you think they'll do to me if they know who we are?"

"You are engaged maybe?" the man beside me was saying. "Or honey-mooning?" His voice was almost too solicitous.

I turned away from him in despair, and walked over to where she had motioned. A chair in front of the now almost extinct fire? An astral lamp that stood on a table? While pondering thus and patching these rich fragments, I, strolling up to the mantel-piece perceived, nestling between the ormolu timepiece and a vase of early primroses, a snuff box!

I took it up and examined it eagerly, admiring the choice and rare design. It glowed there with the radiant glory of rare old gold; and the image and the letters stood out in high relief, clear and sharp.

So, this was it, this was the cloud that brooded over. This was the termination of an ungoverned curiosity, an impulse that I had represented to myself as so innocent or so venial.

"Right ho," I said, and started for the open door to the porch beyond, sauntering at first in a languid sort of way, like a connoisseur a bit bored at having his time wasted.

I say "at first," because I had only taken a couple of steps when I tripped over the cat, and you can't combine tripping over cats with languid sauntering. Shifting abruptly into high, I shot out of the door like someone wanted by the police making for the car after a smash-and-grab raid. The snuff box flew from my hands, and it was a lucky thing that I happened to barge into a fellow citizen outside, or I should have taken a toss off the porch and down the lawn.

Well, not absolutely lucky, as a matter of fact, for it turned out to be Prince Paradox. He stood there goggling at me and the box with horror and indignation behind the pince-nez.

"Get him, Dan! Get him!" he cried, skipping like the high hills.

Dan the Dictator sprang to the task, flying about in excitement.

Some time later, someone was shaking my shoulder. "Wake up!"

"Le'me lone!"

"You've got to wake up. Please wake up."

I groaned inwardly.

"Yes, my Hero—please!"

I opened my eyes then tried to look around. The crowd was still there; it had, indeed, increased. And then it hit me. The whole thing hit me. The snuff box was gone. Catherine was gone. Sure enough, by then all was lost, and darkness overwhelmed.

Kee-ripes, what a shambles!

XXII

BEING THE TYPO-TORTURED TALE OF MY TIME FOLLOWING THE LOSS OF THE SNUFF BOX

As if some awful composite of grief had broke through from the preterite world I kept on sitting there. I didn't even light a cigarette.

I continued to sit here for quite a while as their cried filled the night. The Tall Man still hovering over the crowod. Jennifer still trying to do as Raul had instructed, and see what he was so eager she saw. Lovemakig had warmed them, and the fire crackled cheerfully in the land of lost of time.

But within an hours, the crowd began to detach itself, to assume ameboid shape. Xaxier let go Ollie's hand, leaed over to rub Vernon. (Arnold hd been passed over.) As thing turned out, Xaxier went directly to me, pouring himself from the sinister bottle of half-tumblerful of his mixture (he'd meant to pur the whiskey).

"Oh, I'll find you some," said West.

"Magnifico," said Xaxier, with a gesture at me as if he to say "Oh magic moment that are so perfect, unknown, inevitable."

A man sitting next him, Sing, smiled cordially to his fellow-travelers and leaned back in his seat, picking his teeth with tip of his Bowie knife. His feet barley touching the ground. I gave him an inkling of what Yvette, his wife, had said to me who have no charioteer nor box: "I'm dumber that an eight-year-old. I ought to back and face the music."

The Man just went on picking big horseteeth.

Someone was sitting next him with his back half turned. His hair, swept back behind his ears, was so blond that it was white. He lit a new cigarette form the one he'd been smoking and called out to me: "You are to critical. Do not be soo foolish as to imagine you have no object, no box. Everyting comes in due time."

It was away past the time for any it; these guy poisoning the world with their hope and courage. "*Now* I guelss I can get over it . . ." sad I sarcasticly.

"Want see the positive side of things?" Sing sad pointing to the man who stood quietly by. "It maybe that he will have some suggestion to make that will be of value."

The young man with the long wite hair: "True! I have see this. In the unhopeful light of the moon's arival, when the white men stepped up and took the box from your trembling fingers in the *terra cognito of* the porch, only then did the Dictator hurry back inside, carefully shutting the door and, like a practised architect, started to study it."

I noded.

"But then he had to stop. He beheld a beautifl man lying stretched at full length on table; he felt as if the beating of his heart must suffocate him. The man placed the box in a bag upon a chair on the premise and introduced himself to him, leaping, very bold and impudent, to the table itself. Left to themselves, they could go on this way forever, harmoniously abandoning themselves to the rhythm of the music—like two small chips being tossed about on a rough but friendly sea."

The old feeding of gaiety and bliss was so quick, a joy so strong it might be measured in a language of angelic orders, of powers and dominations, decadence and immortality. How could I possibly belive it? And yet, on the other hand, were not my suspicions antennae pointing in the direction of the truth? "Which which chair, my dear good Man? Lounging-chair? Arm-chair? Easy chair?"

“Don’t ask,” he sad. “I’ll starting whining.”

Later that night, when the other people bad gone upstairs to bed, I went and found found the bag and an old saw. Beneath incandescent bulbs (an archaic controlled combusion of filaments), beneath what might originally have been a gun rack in parquetry, but which now held half a dozen narwhale tusks, I took the bag and ripped a hole in it with the was. There was the briefest suspension: my presence (183), the box, and its contents clotted together.

No so long after that, the guard returned and he was flabbergasted to hear than the bag was missing. Hie pipe was lit and flopping about. “Bearded idots!” His voice had taken on a edge of bitterness. He cursed his stupidity in having let it pass out of his possession. He listend, looking like a jaunty, sudoriferous and and agora-compulsive younger brother. He certain wished he knew who these sinister forces were . . .

From the bruise-colored shadows, I tugged on the gown and sleeves I’d discarded like a wonton. Tormented by my own ghosts, as if the net that hold my wide-eyes open hung over a swamp of junk, I stood back back from the man holding the flintlock. His eyes found found me incomplete bewilderment: “If is you, isn’t it?”

“Wbo?”

“Who ideed.” He had himse;f a hyena laugh.

His imperturbability My heart and knowing. The the terrible feeding would not go away. As with all gut feelings, only time will tell whether this it was the moment in which I did anything so revolutionary as a hot dog in Oxford Street. In order escape, I did it. Took it on as a challenge and I did it: Man went to the ground. “Mister!” he pleased. Man went to the ground right out his shoes. Struck him three or four blows on his shoulders and an equal number of times on the ground. It was a mean thing thing to do, but is was as it he had become invisible (was sprawled on a kind of nest, apparently asleep).

With the utmost care, I carried the object, all dented, to the balcony. I stood drawing long signs of icy relief, saw that the sky was more vast that an unmappable operational endlessless; that moonlight night heavenly, wonderful, miraculus.

XXIII

BEING THE SHORT SHORT STORY OF WHAT HAPPENED THE NEXT MORNING WHEN THE SUN HAD NOT YET RISEN

When I awoke the next morning, it seemed as if all the events of the preceding evening had been a dream, and nothing but the identity of the ancient chamber convinced me of their reality. The sun had not yet risen, and the air was piercingly cold; the grey light, however, of dawn enabled me to distinguish objects with tolerable accuracy. Judd was out of bed and busily dressing. Old Nuflo was already among the ashes, on his hands and knees, blowing the embers he had uncovered to a flame. Then Rima appeared only to pass through the room with a quick light tread to go out of the door without a word or even a glance.

The sun had not yet risen, but already the air was warmer and more alive. I soon heard the clattering of the Nibelung Alberich. The Rhine-maidens, guardians of the gold, were frolicking around it; but this did not appear, for the sun had not yet risen to wake it into radiance. Still the sun had not yet risen when Drost Peter (aka Prince Paradox), with the twelve house-carls, returned, and, entering the chamber, he held up the lantern so that its rays might fall upon the sleeping snuff box bandits. Stepping softly, so as not to waken them, he touched Tatters on the shoulder, with fingers to his lips, motioned for him to come and tiptoed after him.

Then I realized everything. The sun had not yet risen; the dawn—milk-white, without a trace of pink, clean, the air sharp—stood at the window. In this earliest light, Lester passed among the sleeping comrades with a shake on the shoulder for each. I began to feel that it was time for me to go. So I rose from my couch, donned my pelisse, and grabbed the box, and, though the sun had not yet risen, I left my snoring bed-fellow to his slumbers and resumed my journey.

Though the Sun had not yet risen, I found a bright little Fire already kindled in the Parlour, and the little oval Table drawn close to it, spread for Breakfast, with strong Tea and hot Toast awaiting me on the Hob. The room smelled very sweet, filled with the fragrance of the flowers of the garden. The windows remained wide open. The light was stronger than on the landing, but soft, for the sun had not yet risen.

The sun had not yet risen when the Secretary of the Treasury, Salmon P. Chase, entered the room. The door was standing wide open, admitting the cold, and the world shivered in the cold beginning of day. The sun had not yet risen but was still resting somewhere behind the hills.

XXIV

BEING A VISUAL RENDERING OF MY WALK HOME

LONDON
YORK

XXV

BEING AN OLFACTORY RENDERING OF MY WALK HOME

It was already morning outside. The sun was shining. The earth smelled of moist stones, moss and water. On the wind there already lay a light bouquet of magnolia, hyacinth, daphne and rhododendron . . . but there seemed to be something else besides, something in the garden that gave off a fatally wonderful scent, a scent so exquisite that a nose, a tiny perforated organ, had never before encountered one like it . . .

From the valley a warm wind came up, bearing with it the scent of orange blossoms. It was very warm and almost implausibly still—an undercurrent of warmth waking up the earth. The scent of violets. Green in the air. I walked toward the acacias gracefully.

"Can you smell it?" a man sniffed.

"What?" I said, drawing my finger along my nose and rubbing my eyes.

"There's a smell. Something like caramel, it smells so sweet, so wonderful. Always I am after a scent worthy of this ancient sensibility that will evoke a loving kindness in the heart."

"I avoid sweet scents," I said.

"Like caramel . . . ?" he asked, attempting to find his stern tone.

"Caramel!" I said. "And the smell of pigeons roosting on the kitchen balcony."

He thought for a moment, lifted his head toward the low-hanging flowers and breathed in the scent. In three short, jerky tugs, he snatched up the scent as if it were powder. I could smell the sweetness, but I had to pretend to maintain anonymity.

"My lad," he said. "I want to go to you now, this instant, and ask you to put your nose to my wrist and tell me if I smell of a schoolgirl's pencils, or if I smell of *nard*!"

Just to see, I stuck my nose into it. "Yes! Nard!"

"You are a magician! You have, it appears, a fine nose, young man," he said. "You have a much more sensitive nose than I do. Than anyone I know."

Thanks to the strong absorptive powers of my aunt Léonie's bulbous old-man's nose, I, day in day out since my birth, have smelled more than a passably fine nose. True, he did smell like nard; except I didn't say whether it was done with glue, with soap, with sealing-wax, with sunshine, with leaven, with excrem . . . It would only make matters worse, honestly recalling his olfactory guise. Yes, yes. I considered it all coolly and spoke to himself as follows:

"Will you be kind enough to tell me the direction of —?"

"Certainly," he whispered. "Indeed, you will find it at a short distance from here."

"And what road must I take to go there?"

"You must take the path to your left and follow your nose."

I didn't understand exactly what he meant, but from then on I tried my utmost to let my nose lead me. I lifted it to every step, and then checked the smell of the dirt to see how it responded. In the warm sun, aromatic flakes of resin odour crumbled from the pine-wood, a constant twist in the air, but when I breathed it in I noticed how it got stronger a few inches closer to the south. I caught a bright green scent, falling through the Douglas firs like a waterfall, and tracked it back to the breeze, the way it moved through the tops of the trees, brushing the needles together.

Everyday language would soon prove inadequate for designating all the olfactory notions that arose from certain corners. The forest seemed to disappear. Air mixed with decayed leaves and dried wood wafted out. All the world's fragments were swept up and away, and I, tucked into myself—my nose, my arms and legs all smoothed away—I was no longer smelling mere wood, but kinds of wood: maple-wood, oak-wood, pine-wood, elm-wood, pear-wood, old, young, rotting, mouldering, mossy wood, down to single logs, chips and splinters—and could clearly differentiate them as objects in a way that other people could not have done by sight. All I could think about from then on was becoming a scent hunter. I started climbing up the standing trees, branch by branch, pretending I was Jack the Scent Hunter. Sometimes, clinging high up in the evergreen branches, surrounded by the gentle clacking of their needles, I would catch a tantalizing whiff of something else—a mossy aroma, a sweet burnt smell. Pieces of the fleeting realm of scent. In the period of which we speak, there were strange, rare odors abroad—a tangle of weeds and damp, new-plowed earth, mingled with the heavy perfume of a field of white blossoms somewhere near. But far in the distance a warm tendril of baking bread and somewhere the stinging smell of burning leaves. The scents of a town, of human habitation, domesticity.

Across the road from one hedge to the other brushed a warm wind, laden with the hot greasy scents of frying pancakes and sausages and powdery sweet waffles cooked on the hot plate right there by the roadside; beneath that the sharp, bitter scent of Vianne Rocher's chocolate wafted across the river. I should have known she would be here. The road towards town wakened: the smoke here and there of cooking breakfasts; a scent of wood smoke and something tantalizing, which might be grilling sardines; a faint wake of the grumbling black odor left behind by boats. Yes, yes. I leaned in to smell it but instead smelled the river. Thc air become redolent of a heady mix of river tang and churned earth, and the roses, the scent of roses, purple Burgundy dahlia. The sun now high, the town houses stood of that country order which (just as in certain climes whole tracts of air or ocean are illuminated or scented by myriads of protozoa which we cannot see) fascinate a proper nose with the countless odours springing from their own special virtues, wisdom, habits, a whole secret system of life, invisible, superabundant and profoundly moral, which their atmosphere holds in solution; smells natural enough indeed, and coloured by circumstances as are those of the neighbouring countryside, but already humanised, domesticated, confined, an exquisite, skillful, limpid jelly, blending all the fruits of the season which have left the orchard for the store-room, smells changing with the year, but plenishing, domestic smells, which compensate for the sharpness of hoar frost with the sweet savour of warm bread, smells lazy and punctual as a village clock, roving smells, pious smells; rejoicing in a peace which brings only an increase of anxiety, and in a prosiness which serves as a deep source of poetry, to the stranger who passes through their midst without having lived amongst them. I could smell the sweetness on the air, a damp, fresh smell, the smell of wet asphalt and the odour of dripping woodwork. It was warm; the atmosphere was dank, heavy, tepid. One or two oranges. Five bottles of hot sugarcane juice. And I smelled flowers, the sweet scent of lilies, like in my aunt's garden—and right after it another scent that was not sweet at all but awful, disgusting, like a sewer.

Was it real? I put my hand on the nearest wall, to steady myself. What a stink, at the corner there. I had come upon the scent of the precise point where heaven meets earth. The scent of Eden. And behind it: the mysterious scent of transgression. Metal. Brass, more precisely. Bruised green cardamom. Rushes . . . transgression smells *green.*

The attack of scent had come on too suddenly. For a moment, for a breath, for an eternity it seemed, time was doubled or had disappeared completely. A profoundly sexual scent filled the air, threaded with ghostly wisps of dreams. These wisps were clearly recognizable as scraps of odours. At first they merely floated in thin threads, but then they grew thicker, more cloudlike. And now it seemed as if fog was rising. The fog slowly climbed higher, the city-borne breeze damp and acrid, still damp with dread after all of this time. The stink of mud and slime. And then a little human odour. But it remained very vague and masked, was more the suggestion of general exhalations than a personal odour.

The odour came rolling down the rue like a ribbon, unmistakably clear, and after a few steps, what little wind wafted through was swallowed by the tall buildings with grey courtyards, interminable corridors and a smell of rank medicaments, which did not exactly inspire liveliness. The rivers stank, the marketplaces stank, the churches stank, it stank beneath bridges and palaces.

I scurried along in a blur of amazement, wonder and the beginnings of fear, past delights and horrors: The sharp burn of cordite in the air and the smell of hot dogs and frying onions and the faint whiff of garbage. The narrow streets drifted with a claustrophobic stankiness. Farther the streets smelled of new soap and then, suddenly, stank of manure, the courtyards, of urine. The stench of sulphur rose from the chimneys, the stench of caustic lyes from the tanneries, and from the slaughterhouses came the stench of congealed blood, a certain bad smell that was supposed to have some connection with a rash upon the children's faces.

As I descended and rebounded, but so slowly! in my well of smell and every sense of human countenance, every human being smelled. People stank of sweat and unwashed clothes; from their mouths came the stench of rotting teeth, from their bellies that of onions, and from their bodies, if they were no longer very young, came the stench of rancid cheese and sour milk and tumorous disease. A strong stifling odor pervaded the mob scene that stunk with liquor, tobacco smoke and wine smells. The whiff of the great city's vice caught in this manner sent a little tremor of pleasure and excitement over all my dismal, my *dubious* influence! I lifted my fingers to my face to smell them because I thought for the first time (and too late!) that my fingers must smell of the terrible and wonderful scent of vanished times.

Farther I caught glimpses of the flat brown river. By the waterside there was a mellow stink of sewage and rot. Around another corner into an even more crowded street, narrow, lined with tall wooden buildings, between them, I caught a whiff of odorous burnt lard, one that smelled too much of pig, sheep or cow. The street smelled of its usual smells: water, faeces, rats and vegetable matter; lamb kidney toasting on open fires. A scent might be *milky* or *metallic, sulphurous* or *chalky.* One smelled of *old silver* and yet another was *symphonic*—unlike stenches my rivals call perfume but which are no better than the urine of asses and camels!

I let the air into my nose, passed shop fronts where bloody meat hung on enormous hooks, or vegetables and fruit were set out in gleaming rows, or a smell of fresh bread wafted out of hidden ovens, passed a door with a bush dried over it, and the stale smell of ale strong from inside. A greasy aroma drifted down from the third floor—spare ribs and Cinnabons . . . ripe cherry. No sooner had the most attuned nose of them all smelled the scent, the air smelling more of perfume, than I ran straight into Roper, and he threw his arms around me.

He smelled terrible, because of having thrown up. I guess he knew that, since he let me go almost at once, but he stood there looking at me very seriously, a small man of about thirty, blond, with a bulbous nose, short limbs, flat, cheesy feet, swollen genitalia, choleric temperament and a stale mouth odor—not a handsome man, aromatically speaking, this sackmaker. The smell of plump unwashed flesh and unfresh clothing—that odor of unfastidious sedentation, of static overflesh not enough bathed—spread and made captives of the people all around.

Down the street the ground-floor windows appeared where there were gaps in the crowd. Squawking crows and ravens hopped and pecked and fought over garbage in the ditch which led down to the side door of home, our space, my space. The tract which separated it from me could yet be reached by a circuit, by a digression, were I to take the plain, terrestrial path. When I reached the door, it smelled quite clearly like the doorknob, though very faintly, of home.

Ah, returning home was pleasant! The air did not smell of car exhaust but of long-simmered lamb and fresh coffee, the comforting smell of animal dung and old bacon grease. Certainly if you stuck your nose into some of the other neighborhood households you could smell far worse things.

Three steps in from the door, the room took on the scent of mastic; in the kitchen, spoiled cabbage and mutton fat; the unaired parlour stank of stale dust from inert objects: stone, metal, glass, wood, salt, water, air . . . What before had been our space, my space, a kind of home was now blended into a stale smell . . . like something I had smelled before, but I couldn't think what, or when.

The guests thronged around. "Hello! are you here *again*?"

"Do you want any assistance?" asked Moira B before stepping back, holding her nose between thumb and finger.

She laughed delightedly and took my hand, called to Clemence.

Clemence, having folded over the back of the chair with her head bent, sniffed disdainfully, almost choking into my hand.

"Oh! La, la. What a stench!" said Clemence, holding her nose. "Do you have a clothes pin?" And then she went off.

"It smells all right," I said casually to Gil.

Becoming aware of the smell, he sat up a little. Straightening up, he was struck with a humid waft of boiled hot dogs and some kind of furry bean-based soup that threw him right back into tenth grade.

"How ridiculously bad the scent!" he said after a long pause. The very longdrawn pitch of his voice seemed to smell of whiskey.

"Shut it!" So I said.

He did not move and his voice was not raised: "These exhibitions are absurd. Go on upstairs."

His phrases irritated me; I was about to retort sharply. But his expression became so eloquent of distress, that I relented. And so I set forth. *So I smell of the shit of a fabled creature,* I thought, *must climb each step of the staircase "against my heart," as the saying is, climbing in opposition to my heart's desire.*

That hateful staircase, up which I always passed with such dismay, gave out a smell of varnish which had to some extent absorbed, made definite and fixed the special quality of sorrow that I felt each evening, and made it perhaps even more cruel to my sensibility because, when it assumed this olfactory guise, my intellect was powerless to resist it.

I crept upstairs, trembling all over. The smell of charred pastry crust filled the corridor. It was a wonderful smell and soothing. It made me sick that I had to go to bed—such wonderful things in the air, a brighter scent of milk and cheesy wool. I put the box down on the dresser and sat on the edge of the bed which smelled of apples, camphor, freshly lacquered furniture. It was a pleasant aroma, so that for several instants I closed my eyes and slept.

When I awoke, something extraordinary happened. I saw in the well of the stair a light coming upwards. For a few moments, the miracle of its apparition seemed glidingly to mount the wall, and tremblingly to pause in the centre of the obscured ceiling. I lifted up my head to look: a gentleman came out and hurried up the steps.

Fortunately I had my glasses with me, and then I saw at once that it was a nose, full size, so to speak, in the doorway, his legs slightly apart, his arms slightly spread. This nose moved, pushed upwards and sniffed. It sucked air in and snorted it back out in short puffs, like an imperfect sneeze. Then the nose wrinkled up, seemed to fix on a particular target: me.

XXVI

BEING THE DISCREET DREAMS OF THE BOURGEOISIE

"What are you?" I asked.

"I'm more astonished than wot you are," said the nose.

The eyes slitted open. I yawned.

"What do you smell?" he persisted. He was emphatic, dictatorial, chain-smoking heavily, proclaiming amidst a fog of thick smoke that he was the only real nose left in the city. "That is my profession. I am a 'nose,' as they say."

"Mr. Nose! Ah, I'll get it this time," I said grimly.

The intruder appeared to hesitate, and muttered to himself. At last, he said, in a half-whisper, plainly not expecting an answer, "Can't sleep?"

"I almost was, and then I woke up."

"You are indeed the Sleeper," he said. "I saw you asleep. There's a Kafka story about a man who woke up one morning and found he had turned into a giant cockroach. It horrifies everybody that one, the idea of being turned into a cockroach—but if he'd really wanted to sick people off Kafka should have made the guy into a wood-louse."

I was making an effort to reform the concept when he let out a smeck, viddying me.

And then I woke up, as I always do where I started actually, and everything's just the way it was. No nose any more! The room was just a room, small, lit by one stump of candle.

I went to the bathroom to brush my teeth. My toothbrush, paste, and water glass were crowded as usual onto a shelf. As I glanced into the bathroom mirror for a moment, the shelf on which all these things rested started to tilt. My water glass slid slowly along it, then fell and broke on the tile into thick, sharp pieces. I lost my balance, slipped, and stepped directly onto a shard of glass. Blood filled the floor. My family came. I was crying, sobbing. "I'm sorry," I said, "I cannot give you any more presents. I love you all, but I don't want to give you any more presents." The words came flying out of my mouth. I didn't know why I was saying them. I'd always wanted them to have the best of everything.

Then I woke up and thought about the dream, the presents. I thought about Christmas, the streets, the shops. "Comme c'est terrible," I said, "quelle chance que ça s'est fait la nuit!" I lay there a little sick, looking at shadows on the white plaster ceiling. I remembered a long time ago when I lay in bed beside my mother, watching lights from the street move across the ceiling and down the walls.

Then I woke up and there you were. You were in this huge house that was like a maze, walking around, searching for some special room, but you couldn't find it. There was somebody else in the house, looking for you. I tried to yell a warning, but you couldn't hear me.

When I woke up, I was in a foundry and there was an enormous vat of red, bubbling, liquid iron they'd just drawn off the furnace, and you came down from the ceiling on a spider web and hung over it.

And then I woke up, and I was covered with cold sweat—for fear the web wouldn't break. My clothes were soaked through with sweat. My eyes were watering and smarting. My whole body felt itchy and irritable. I twisted about on the bed, arching my back and stretching my arms and legs.

Then I woke up again and fell asleep again. I was on the sea. I felt so faint that I barely had the strength to catch the new smell of ropes and tar. It was cool in the heaving niche where I was lying directly under a wide-open porthole. They'd left me alone. Evidently my journey was continuing . . . But what journey? I heard steps on the deck, a wooden deck right over my nose, and voices, and the waves lashing and melting against the ship's side.

And then I woke up, for the train stopped at the place where the tickets are collected; and, in another five minutes, I was in a cab, with my bag and the great basket of country treasures, creeping along in the early November morning towards Gray's Inn Lane.

Then I woke up and I was here, lying on a sofa, a sofa covered with a curious sort of hard, shiny material with a red and black pattern on it, and I was screaming, but I do not know why I screamed. I got up and changed my underwear, locked the office and left.

At the end of the corridor, in the angle of the wall, a youngish blond man in a brown suit and a cocoa-colored straw hat with a brown and yellow tropical print band was reading the evening paper with his back to the wall. As I passed him he yawned and tucked the paper under his arm and straightened up.

He got into the elevator with me. He said in a thick, uncertain voice:

"John, my boy, I had a dream last night. I dreamt I tried some of them high spots yonder. I struck the rock with my pick, and suddenly I was dazzled. Wet flakes of shining gold stared up at me from the quartz. I struck again, and there was more gold. I struck right and left, and a perfect shower of nuggets as big as my head rolled at my feet. Then I woke up."

"Yes, then you woke up," I said, swallowing to keep the misery out of my voice, "like seawater and river water flowing together. I struggle to find the meaning behind it all, but nothing makes sense."

Just then I yawned, and then . . . I woke up and it was all dark and my head achin' fit to split. I presume I went to sleep again . . .

But then I woke up in the hospital, and I was coming down with rabies. I looked in the mirror and my face changed and I began howling.

Then I woke up, and sure as you live, I was being run over by a steam roller.

Then I woke up. It wasn't me. It was somebody else. Angel was killed by the sun. Incinerated. Vaporized. Whatever. The scene was unreal and flat and pointless, as though I'd forced my way into someone else's dream.

Then I woke up to find the sun streaming in at my window. And, of course, it was that bright sun shining on my face that caused the dream. I heard a most wonderful melody and suddenly I realized it was getting louder and louder every second!

Then I woke up to what was happening: those damn geese!

But when I woke up I found that I was sleeping near a strawstack and was listening to the braying of a jackass.

Then I woke up real skorry, my heart going bap bap bap, and of course there was really a bell going brrrrr, and it was our front-door bell. I let on that nobody was at home, but this brrrrr still ittied on, and then I heard a goloss shouting through the door: "Come on then, get out of it, I know you're in bed." I recognized the goloss right away. It was the goloss of P. R. Deltoid (a real gloopy nazz, that one) what they called my Post-Corrective Adviser, an overworked veck with hundreds on his books.

When I awaked, it was just day-light. I attempted to rise, but was not able to stir: for, as I happened to lie on my back, I found my arms and legs were strongly fastened on each side to the ground. I likewise felt several slender ligatures across my body, from my arm-pits to my thighs. In a little time I felt something alive moving on my left leg, which advancing gently forward over my breast, came almost up to my chin; when, bending my eyes downwards as much as I could, I perceived it to be a human creature not six inches high, with a box in his hands. "That's the same box you took, isn't it," I said to my self. "This creature is planning some new outrage, some fresh deviltry or other." The man was none other than Prince Paradox himself! I was in the utmost astonishment, and roared so loud that I woke up thinking of the word "divisive."

And then I woke up and it was the middle of the night and I was all right. I was in bed at home. Only it wasn't any home I'd ever had, the other time, the first time. The bad time. Oh God, I wish I didn't remember it. I mostly don't. I can't. I've told myself ever since that it was a dream. That it was a dream! But it wasn't. This is. This isn't real. This world isn't even probable. It was the truth. It was what happened. We are all dead, and we spoiled the world before we died. There is nothing left. Nothing but dreams.

XXVII

BEING THE AWKWARD ACCOUNT OF MY CONFRONTATION WITH PRINCE PARADOX

Then I woke up here in the middle of a room full of people. A ball. I am not going to describe that ball. Everything about it was just as it always is. There was a band, with trumpets extraordinarily out of tune, in the gallery; there were country gentlemen, greatly flustered, with their inevitable families, mauve ices, viscous lemonade; servants in boots trodden down at heel and knitted cotton gloves; provincial lions with spasmodically contorted faces, and so on and so on. And all this little world was revolving round its sun—round the Prince himself, who stood straight, tall and fair. Lost in the crowd, unnoticed even by the young ladies of eight-and-forty, with red pimples on their brows and blue flowers on the tops of their heads, I stared incessantly, first at the prince, then at Catherine (Catherine!!) then at the snuff box (the snuff box!!??) in his hands, grim and terrible in the ghostly radiance that fell upon it.

The prince turned to me and, probably incited by the goose-like expression of my face, made me a deep bow. This sarcastic bow transmitted to me through my triumphant rival, his careless smile, all this lashed me to frenzy . . . I moved up to the prince and whispered furiously, "You think fit to laugh at me, it seems?"

The prince looked at me with contemptuous surprise, took my arm, and making a show of re-conducting me to my seat, answered coldly, "I?"

"Yes, you!" I went on in a whisper, obeying, however—that is to say, following him to my place; "you; I do not intend to permit any empty-headed Petersburg up-start——"

The prince smiled tranquilly, almost condescendingly, pressed my arm, whispered, "I understand you." The prince took my arm and led me apart.

"You, I believe," he began, emphasizing the word "you," and looking at my chin with a contemptuous expression, which, strange to say, was supremely becoming to his fresh and handsome face, "you said something abusive to me?"

"I said what I thought," I replied, raising my voice. "Leave me in peace! Leave Catherine! And give it to me now—the snuff box which you took. Give it up, and you can go at your convenience. But I must have it—even if I am obliged to drive you to the limit. I advise you to save yourself much suffering, and give it to me now!"

"Sh . . . quietly," he observed; "decent people don't bawl."

"Give it to me. Otherwise I will take measures! I will fight!"

"Now I understand. You would like, perhaps, to fight me?" he said, smiling. "He would like to entertain himself with a duel. I can grant him the satisfaction. Mr., I accept your challenge."

My heart was thumping at my ribs. "*Challenge?* Well . . . er, er, er . . . I, don't you see, I usually don't . . . you see . . . I'm against bloodshed . . . And what's more, I, er . . . there's the law to consider . . ."

The prince took my arm. "I *am* the law here, my man. I have the honour to lay the following proposition before you: the combat to take place tomorrow, let us say, in the grove known as 'The Oaks,' located 3½ miles from town, with pistols, at a distance of ten paces . . ."

"At ten paces? that will do; we hate one another at that distance."

"We might have it eight," he laughed.

"We might," I snarled.

“To fire twice; and, to be ready for any result, let each put a letter in his pocket, in which he accuses himself of his end.”

“Now, that I don’t approve of at all.” I, as it were, twitched all over. “There’s a slight flavour of the French novel about it, something not very plausible.”

“Perhaps. You will agree, however, that it would be unpleasant to incur a suspicion of murder?”

“I agree as to that . . .”

The prince smiled tranquilly, almost condescendingly, pressed my arm, whispered, “Two by two is four, a rock is a rock. Tomorrow, lo and behold, we’re having a duel. You and I will say that it’s foolish and absurd, that the duel has outlived its era, that in reality the aristocratic duel in no way differs from a drunken brawl in a tavern, but still we will not disengage, will go and will fight.”

I replied, raising my voice: “So be it. Au revoir—tomorrow.”

XXVIII

BEING THE DAY OF THE DUEL

I could not sleep all night—from excitement, not from cowardice. I am not a coward. I positively thought very little of the possibility confronting me of losing my life. I could think only of Catherine and the box, of my ruined hopes, of what I ought to do. "Ought I to try to kill the prince?" I asked myself; and, of course, I wanted to kill him—not from revenge, but from a desire for the box and Catherine's good. "But she will not survive such a blow," I went on. "No, better let him kill me!" I must own it was an agreeable reflection, too, that I, an obscure provincial person, had forced a man of such consequence to fight a duel with me.

The morning light found me still absorbed in these reflections; and, not long after it, appeared Koloberdyaev, a cavalry captain in the Uhlans and my second. He announced to me that "we're going to fight to-day at three o'clock with pistols." In silence I bent my head, in token of my agreement.

At two o'clock we had lunch, and at three we were at the place fixed upon—the very birch copse in which I had once walked with Catherine. An immense crowd of people, for whom benches and platforms had been put up, had filled the soft ground between the trees! It was too much. Almost all the knights of Swabia and Switzerland were present on the sloping terrace.* And at the same time, surrounded by his courtiers, sat the Emperor himself, together with his consort.

* They sat wearing very large whiskers and magnificent *homeward-bounders*—so they called the long fly-brushes at their chins—and endless *goatees* and *imperials;* and what with abounding

Shortly before the beginning of the fight, George Lamil remembered Baron de Vaux's book upon experts with the pistol, and he ran through it from one end to the other. Officer Boyko retrieved two pistols from a case, and the knights stood there, arguing about ceremony.

We arrived first; but the prince and Bizmyonkov did not keep us long waiting. The prince was, without exaggeration, as fresh as a rose; his brown eyes looked out with excessive cordiality from under the peak of his cap. He was smoking a cigar, playing with the box, and on seeing Koloberdyaev shook his hand in a friendly way.

Even to me he bowed very genially. I was conscious, on the contrary, of being pale, and my hands, to my terrible vexation, were slightly trembling . . . my throat was parched . . . I had never fought a duel before. "O God!" I thought; "if only that ironical gentleman doesn't take my agitation for timidity!" I was inwardly cursing my nerves; but glancing, at

---

locks, others of the crew seemed a company of Merovingians or Long-haired kings, mixed with savage Lombards or Longobardi, so called from their lengthy beards. In particular, the more aged sported most venerable beards of an exceeding length and hoariness, like long, trailing moss hanging from the bough of some aged oak there. The two long, even lines of beards seemed one dense grove. Nodding harvests! Whiskerandoes! Vinyl locks! Worshipped beards! The fleece! Above all, the Captain, old Ushant—a fine specimen of a sea sexagenarian—wore a wide, spreading beard, grizzled and grey, that flowed over his breast and often became tangled and knotted with tar. He was a sort of a sea-Socrates, in his old age; and I never could look at him, and survey his right reverend beard, without bestowing upon him that title which, in one of his satires, Persius gives to the immortal quaffer of the hemlock—*Magister Barbatus*—the bearded master. Not a few of the company had also bestowed great pains upon their hair, which some of them—especially the genteel young bucks of the After-guard—wore over their shoulders like the ringleted Cavaliers. Many, with naturally tendril locks, prided themselves upon what they call *love curls,* worn at the side of the head, just before the ear—a custom peculiar to tars, and which seems to have filled the vacated place of the old-fashioned Lord Rodney cue, which they used to wear some fifty years ago. But there were others labouring under the misfortune of long, lank, Winnebago locks, carroty bunches of hair, or rebellious bristles of a sandy hue. Ambitious of redundant mops, these still suffered their carrots to grow, spite of all ridicule. They looked like Huns and Scandinavians; and one of them, a young Down Easter, the unenvied proprietor of a thick crop of inflexible yellow bamboos, went by the name of *Peter the Wild Boy.* But there were many fine, flowing heads of hair to counter-balance such sorry exhibitions as Peter's.

last, straight in the prince's face, and catching on his lips an almost imperceptible smile, I suddenly felt furious again, and was at once at my ease. Meanwhile, our seconds were fixing the barrier, measuring out the paces, loading the pistols. Koloberdyaev did most, loaded the pistols with the skill of a veteran duelist; Bizmyonkov rather watched him, looked round, and remarked: "Poor ground."

"It's unfit," replied the cavalry officer.

The prince proceeded: "Why bother about ground, measurements, and so on? Let us simplify matters. Load the two pistols."

"I will," called Koloberdyaev.

I swallowed.

The prince went on smoking his cigar, leaning with his shoulder against the trunk of a young lime-tree . . .

"Kindly take your places, gentlemen; ready," Koloberdyaev pronounced at last, handing us pistols.

The prince walked a few steps away, stood still, and, turning his head, asked me over his shoulder, "You still refuse to take back your words, then?"

I tried to answer him; but my voice failed me, and I had to content myself with a contemptuous wave of the hand.

At a nod from the Emperor the herald then sounded the signal for the fight to begin. The prince smiled again, and took up his position in his place. The crowd of officers cheered; up at the trees, the little birds singing sanely.

We began to approach one another as the crowd began to cheer and hoot. "Fire!" cried Mavriky Nikolaevitch in extreme agitation. "Fire!" cried Stavrogin, losing all patience. "Impossible!" cried the captain, "fire!" he cried, in a loud, distinct voice. Both university-educated and erudite people called. The hatred!

The prince began to raise his pistol. Silence set in. The crowd was quiet. He aimed right at my forehead . . .

Unutterable fury began to seethe within my breast. I raised my pistol, cocked the hammer, was about to aim at my enemy's chest—but suddenly, in a moment of intense hatred and wrath, tilted it up as though someone had given my elbow a shove, and fired.

A shot rang out. It was the sound of infinitely distant, inconceivable time.

Startled by the report of the pistol, the gulls in a neighbouring cliff flew about screaming.

XXIX

BEING THE SOUNDS THE BIRDS MADE IN THIS FRACTIONAL FRAGMENT OF TIME

NOOOOOOOOOOOoo—! coo roo-hoo hoo! roo-hoo hoo! Cuckoo Cuckoo Cuckoo. Ga Ga Gara! Klook Klook Klook! Gara! Klook Klook Klook! Ga ga ga ga Gara! Klook Klook Klook. Cuckoo Cuckoo Cuckoo. Kaw kave kankury kake. Caw Caw! Caw! Caw! Caw! caw! caw! caw! caw! caw! Ain't I a crow? Who? Whoo? ooraloo— Cuckoo Cuckoo Cuckoo. Hello! Who are you? Tuuu . . . tuu tu tu. Waow! waow! waow! Whip! Whip! Whip-poor-Will! Cuckoo Cuckoo Cuckoo. Honk? Honk. Honk. Honk. Honk! Honk-honk! Honk-honk! aaakk! Cuckoo Cuckoo Cuckoo.

XXX

BEING THE RIVETING RESULTS OF THE DUEL

The prince tottered and put his left hand to his left temple—a thread of blood was flowing down his cheek from under the white leather glove. A number of voices immediately rose up. Bizmyonkov rushed up to him, silenced the other voices with his own powerful bellow.

The prince looked at me with contemptuous surprise. "It's all right," he said, taking off his cap, which the bullet had pierced; "since it's in the head, and I've not fallen, it must be a mere scratch."

He calmly pulled a cambric handkerchief out of his pocket, and put it to his blood-stained curls.

I stared at him, as though I were turned to stone, and did not stir.

"Go up to the barrier, if you please!" Koloberdyaev observed severely.

I obeyed.

"Is the duel to go on?" he added, addressing Bizmyonkov.

Bizmyonkov made him no answer. But the prince, without taking the handkerchief from the wound, without even giving himself the satisfaction of tormenting me at the barrier, replied with a smile, "The duel is at an end," and fired into the air. "Foolish man!" cried his mother. "Impossible!" cried the captain, "impossible!" I was almost crying with rage and vexation. This man by his magnanimity had utterly trampled me in the mud; he had completely crushed me. I was on the point of making objections, on the point of demanding that he should fire at me. But he came up to me, and held out his hand.

"It's all forgotten between us, isn't it?" he said in a friendly voice, showing me the box.

I looked at his blanched face, at the blood-stained handkerchief, and utterly confounded, put to shame, and annihilated, I pressed his hand, took the box from trembling fingers and examined it carefully.

The prince, as he went away, bowed to me once more. But Bizmyonkov did not even glance at me. Shattered—morally shattered—I went homewards with Koloberdyaev, which invariably roused the crowd to go home.

"Why, what's the matter with you?" the cavalry captain asked me. "Set your mind at rest; the wound's not serious. He'll be able to dance by tomorrow, if you like. Or are you sorry you didn't kill him? You're wrong, if you are; he's a first-rate fellow."

"What business had he to spare me!" I muttered at last.

"Oh, so that's it!" the cavalry captain rejoined tranquilly . . . "Ugh, you writing fellows are too much for me!"

I don't know what put it into his head to consider me an author.

XXXI

BEING THE GOLDEN PRELUDE TO AN ENDING

I started to reply, but a sudden burst of military music drowned my voice. It was my cousin's regiment. They were a fine lot of fellows, in their pale, tight-fitting jackets, jaunty busbys and riding breeches with the double yellow stripe, into which their limbs seemed moulded. Every other squadron was armed with lances, from the metal points of which fluttered yellow and white pennons. The band passed, playing the regimental march; then came a barrow full of yellow jonquils and white Roman hyacinths in a golden cloud of mimosa.

There are so many things which are impossible to explain! Why should certain chords in music make me think of the brown and golden tints of autumn foliage? Why should the Mass of Sainte Cécile bend my thoughts wandering among rough oak? I was mechanically fussing with the box, lost in these golden thoughts, when the amber light quit blinking in my eyes. Something marvellous appeared to me:

Nearby, the regiment trod out the shattering dance music with serene patience. Locked together, Gombauld and Anne moved with a harmoniousness that made them seem a single creature, two-headed and four-legged. Mr. Scogan, solemnly buffoonish, shuffled round with Mary. I looked, and there to my right Catherine sat in the shadows scribbling, so it seemed, in a thick yellow notebook. Her short hair, clipped like a page's, hung in a bell of elastic gold about her cheeks.

Catherine looked up; her hair swung back, a soundless bell of gold. Her eyes were serene; she smiled. So the moment had come; a face appeared and coalesced into one of them lemony, tight-lipped smiles of hers.

"You have exposed my poor strategy," she said. Then, after a pause, she fixed her eyes for a moment upon a small sunspot; then she got up. At that moment, on the branch of an acacia, just over her head, a goldfinch began to sing his thin, sweet, crystalline trill of song.

"I think I must tell you . . ." she continued with a sigh and did not conceal the fact that she had been obliged to get rid of the Prince to protect the box. The box was of no consequence, though: "Inside that box is another still smaller of metal and that contains the secret of the whole device."

"What's the secret? I think you might tell me!"

"Don't you see?" she asked wistfully. She took the box and opened it now. What I saw was the shimmer of sunlight on metal. Nothing else? Nothing.

She noticed my keen disappointment.

"Cheer up," she said; "the box is on its road home. To-night its rightful owner will end the whole thing. And," she closed the box, and the tears were in her eyes, "it will end up like a story too, and, please God, live happy ever after."

She took my hand between hers and smiled up at me. She took the box and hurried back to the golden gates of Fairy-land, where the woods and forests were always full of daffodils and buttercups and black-eyed Susans.

We left the crowds behind, and the broader avenues were spanned by the open sky. My grievances melted away, and I fell to dreaming of things that neither hurt nor pleased. A fringe of trees against the sun became suddenly the symbol of the whole world, and I stood and gazed and asked questions of it. I was drowsy with the fresh air, half drugged with the pungent, lemony, resinous odour of the pines.

When we reached the gates of Fairy-land, it was late in the afternoon. In front was a big gate, all studded with gemstones and everywhere the fair stories told as if they were verily alive.

There was a bell beside the gate. Catherine pushed the button and heard a silvery tinkle sound within. Then the big gate swung slowly open, and a land of scented gardens opened before us.

I gazed overhead. Was it—compared to my stature—four times what it was? The gate was very high and wide, yet it had such a narrow entranceway that two men or two horses could scarcely enter abreast.

Beyond the gate the road descended gradually through an open pasture, where sheep grazed on the hillside or lay at rest in the shade. The bells of the leaders tinkled faintly, the ewes and the lambs were calling. There were several roads nearby, but it did not take long to find the one paved with yellow bricks.

XXXII

BEING THE END OF THIS NOVEL

AND 33 OTHER NOVELS

I took her hand in mine, and we went out of the ruined place; and, as the morning mists had risen long ago, so, the evening mists were rising now, and in all the broad expanse of tranquil light they showed to me, I saw no shadow of another parting from her; I saw the sun rise in a woman's face. For there she was. So we passed through into the cloisters of the forest and out across the dreaming bourns and orchards to the solitary hills.

Peace. All was well. Ebb and flow. Leaving and coming. Flight and fall. Sing and silent. Reaching and reached. Moments. All gathering toward this one. We laughed for a long time, running easily down through the wood, where the first primroses were beginning to bloom. Feet turned towards the right; north, north-east, east, south-east, south, south-south-west; then paused, and, after a few seconds, turned towards the left; south-south-west, south, south-east, east, this way this way this way this way this way this way this way this way this

way out this

way out

O

of the forest, toward the shore. And the ashes blew towards us with the salt wind from the sea. And somewhere the stinging smell of burning leaves. A way a lone a last a loved a long the shore, beyond the barrier cliffs, the great shroud of the sea rolled on as it rolled five thousand years ago.

The sea. The earth. The house of the seven gables toward the shore. It was the end of the line. It was the beginning of my present prosperity. It was an adventure. The beginning of an adventure. That was how it felt. So that, in the end, there was no end. This was just the beginning. It was not midnight. It was not raining. Evening began to fall.

We sat there for a long time, till the sun shifted and the light changed. Till we felt our eyes could meet again, without the tears. Then the sky began to change colour, subtly and slowly at first, then faster and wilder than anyone could dream. Catherine was the first to get up and stretch out her body as the dusk fell rapidly westwards.

We stayed out in the garden of the old house until we couldn't see to kick a ball, laughing in the gathering twilight, making the most of the good weather and all the days that were left, our little game watched only by next door's cat, and every star in the heavens. Birds flew chittering and their long shadows passed in tandem like the shadow of a single being. Passed and paled into the darkening land, the world to come.

I took one more glance over my past life, then turned to the future. I was eager to embrace the world. I began making my way back to my seat. "Now I know that our world is no more permanent than a wave rising on the ocean. Whatever our struggles and triumphs, however we may suffer them, all too soon they bleed into a wash, just like watery ink on paper."

"Ex hac luce," she said, as though speaking to herself, "out of this light; alas! alas! for some the light is darkness."

"Yes," I said. "Isn't it pretty to think so?"

And Catherine kept squinting until finally, smiling gratefully, she answered, "Yes. Yes—yes—yes . . ." Three words only remained, and she spoke them with all her heart. "I love you."

I could hear my heart beating. I could hear everyone's heart. I could hear the human noise we sat there making, not one of us moving, not even when the room of the world went dark.

"Now I must sleep," I whispered. "I'll pray and then I'll sleep. And so, as Tiny Tim observed, God bless Us, Every One! Amen. And all that cal."

She looked up, and her lips came together and smiled mysteriously. "Lean on me."

I did. And then we fell asleep. And then we continued blissfully into this small but perfect piece of our forever . . .

. . . And then I woke up.

AUTHOR'S NOTE

Apart from the summaries that introduce each chapter, this book contains no words of my own. Through a process of collage and constraint, I have gathered fragments from hundreds of novels and arranged them into a story of love and loss, suspense and snuff boxes.

In several ways, this book was born out of *The Nature Book,* a novel made entirely out of nature descriptions from three hundred other novels. While writing that book and scanning through centuries of literature, I began to notice more patterns, tropes, and clichés in how we compose fiction. For instance, I found four gestures to be ubiquitous in blockbuster novels—nodding, shrugging, odd looks, and gasping—and collaged them into an *Airport Novella* (Troll Thread, 2017). I took first lines from *New Yorker* short stories and turned them into a hybrid story/study of prestige fiction and its imaginative limits ("First Impressions," *BOMB Magazine,* 2018). The more patterns I found, the more I imagined gathering them into a short story collection. That is, until I saw David Hockney's "Nichols Canyon" in person for the first time.

The painting is one of Hockney's most iconic works. It depicts a hilly California landscape composed of radically different textures and colors, each snug against another, and, despite their apparent disparateness, together they form a unified image. I had seen it hundreds of times before—a print of it hung in my parents' office when I was a kid—but when I saw "Nichols Canyon" in person in 2017, something clicked. I realized I could apply this technique—a combination of disparate patterns that form a cohesive, unified work—to fiction. I imagined a novel with each chapter consisting of a radically different pattern, with all the chapters arranged into a continuous story. I immediately thought of this book as a "patchwork" and started to make lists of potential patterns, having no idea what narrative might result.

To name a few: I'd found a lot of premodern novels replacing proper nouns and profanities with em dashes, asterisks, underscores, and ellipses ("the K__ bridge"; "d—mn it!"); I'd noticed multiple books using the same phrase as the first line in Virginia Woolf's *The Waves* ("The sun had not yet risen"); and one of the most glaring and admittedly juvenile observations was the liberal use of "ejaculate" in place of "exclaim" in pre-1900 fiction. After writing a few chapters with these patterns, I found that I'd written the middle of a novel and that my task was then to build out the narrative one chapter, one pattern, at a time: starting from the center and working my way forward and backward toward the beginning and end of the book. I sometimes imagined I was solving a jigsaw puzzle but without a pictorial guide, always looking to the source materials to reveal connections between sentences, paragraphs, scenes, chapters.

In "Nichols Canyon," a winding road both separates and joins the various parts of the painting. I found a similar guiding shape in the hero's journey, the narrative formula identified and popularized by Joseph Campbell in the 1950s. There are many flaws and deserved criticisms that can and have been leveled at Campbell's theory, but the hero's journey is part of our narrative lives whether we like it or not: a version of it can still be found in almost all novels, movies, and even TV shows. The formula goes: A would-be hero rejects a call to adventure, but, with the help of a mentor, inevitably agrees. A journey begins, taking said hero to new lands, introducing them to new friends and foes, launching them into increasingly difficult challenges which become so trying the hero nearly dies, either figuratively or literally. Ultimately, the hero descends into the most dire depths and is reborn, also either figuratively or literally. Victorious, the hero returns home with some sort of boon. Despite the many ways in which this formula falls short (for instance, the hero is often a cis man), it seemed important to allow this most common narrative pattern to shape a book that examines other, smaller narrative patterns. For a full breakdown of how *Patchwork* follows the hero's journey structure, see the following section, which details the sources and patterns used throughout.

SOURCES

Below you will find the patterns and source texts used in each chapter. I have sprinkled four other texts throughout this book given their prolific use of snuff box descriptions (*The Cardinal's Snuff box* by Henry Harland and *The Ivory Snuff box* by Arnold Fredericks) and references to Catherines (*Wuthering Heights* by Emily Brontë and *Catherine* by William Makepeace Thackeray).

I. BEING THE FIRST LINES . . .

GUIDING PATTERN: First lines from novels
PHASE OF HERO'S JOURNEY: "The Ordinary World"

The Absolutely True Diary of a Part-Time Indian, Sherman Alexie
At Swim-Two-Birds, Flann O'Brien
The Bad Beginning, Lemony Snicket
A Bayard from Bengal, Thomas Anstey Guthrie
The Beasts of Tarzan, Edgar Rice Burroughs
The Black Tulip, Alexandre Dumas
Catch-22, Joseph Heller
The Catcher in the Rye, J.D. Salinger
The Chessmen of Mars, Edgar Rice Burroughs
Choke, Chuck Palahniuk
City of Glass, Paul Auster
The Confessions of a Caricaturist, Harry Furniss
A Connecticut Yankee in King Arthur's Court, Mark Twain
Cruddy, Lynda Barry
The Crystal Cave, Mary Stewart
The Curious Incident of the Dog in the Night-Time, Mark Haddon
David Copperfield, Charles Dickens
Dietland, Sarai Walker
The Empty Glass, J. I. Baker
Equality, Edward Bellamy
The Exorcist, William Peter Blatty
The Eyre Affair, Jasper Fforde
A Farewell to Arms, Ernest Hemingway
Finnegans Wake, James Joyce
The Fortress of Solitude, Jonathan Lethem
Galatea 2.2, Richard Powers
The Galaxy Primes, E. E. Smith
The Gloved Hand, Burton Egbert Stevenson
Gulliver's Travels, Jonathan Swift
The Hill of Dreams, Arthur Machen
Hopalong Cassidy's Rustler Round-Up, Clarence E. Mulford
I, Claudius, Robert Graves
Inside, Alix Ohlin

Ishmael, Daniel Quinn
A Knight of the White Cross, G. A. Henty
Life of Pi, Yann Martel
A Little Mother to the Others, L. T. Meade
Looking Backward, Edward Bellamy
The Magus, John Fowles
Many Lives, Many Masters, Dr. Brian Weiss
The Martian, George Du Maurier
Master of the World, Jules Verne
The Night of the Long Knives, Fritz Leiber
Notes from Underground, Fyodor Dostoevsky
On the Road, Jack Kerouac
Oranges Are Not the Only Fruit, Jeanette Winterson
Pale Fire, Vladimir Nabokov
Pharaoh's Broker, Ellsworth Douglass
Murphy, Samuel Beckett
The Prisoner of Zenda, Anthony Hope
The Razor's Edge, W. Somerset Maugham
Riddley Walker, Russell Hoban
Robinson Crusoe, Daniel Defoe
San Miguel, T. C. Boyle
The Secret Life of Bees, Sue Monk Kidd
Siddhartha, Herman Hesse
The Sleeper Awakes, H. G. Wells
A Study in Scarlet, Arthur Conan Doyle
Swann's Way, Marcel Proust
The Swoop!, or How Clarence Saved England, P. G. Wodehouse
A Texas Matchmaker, Andy Adams
That Affair at Elizabeth, Burton Egbert Stevenson
To Kill a Mockingbird, Harper Lee
Uncle Bernac, Arthur Conan Doyle
The Unlikely Pilgrimage of Harold Fry, Rachel Joyce
V., Thomas Pynchon
Walter Sherwood's Probation, Horatio Alger Jr.
We the Animals, Justin Torres
We Were the Mulvaneys, Joyce Carol Oates

II. BEING THE CONTENTS . . .

GUIDING PATTERN: Second-person language from fiction written mostly or entirely in the second person

PHASE OF HERO'S JOURNEY: "The Call to Adventure"

The Bad Beginning, Lemony Snicket
Bright Lights, Big City, Jay McInerney
Complicity, Iain Banks
Half Asleep in Frog Pajamas, Tom Robbins
Halting State, Charles Stross
If on a Winter's Night a Traveler, Italo Calvino
Manon Lescaut, Abbé Prévost
The Night Circus, Erin Morgenstern
The Raven Tower, Ann Leckie
Romeo and/or Juliet, Ryan North

Self-Help, Lorrie Moore
The Sound of My Voice, Ron Butlin
The Subtle Knife, Philip Pullman
Worlds of the Imperium, Keith Laume
You, Austin Grossman

III. BEING MY RESPONSE . . .

GUIDING PATTERN: Nos and synonyms for "no" from books deemed to be the most negative by literary blogs
PHASE OF HERO'S JOURNEY: "Refusal of the Call"

Atonement, Ian McEwan
Bartleby, the Scrivener, Herman Melville
Ethan Frome, Edith Wharton
Less Than Zero, Bret Easton Ellis
Lord of the Flies, William Golding
Jude the Obscure, Thomas Hardy
Never Let Me Go, Kazuo Ishiguro
On the Beach, Neville Shute
Stoner, John Williams
Where the Red Fern Grows, Wilson Rawls
Wuthering Heights, Emily Brontë

FOOTNOTE AND LINE BEFORE THE FOOTNOTE GUIDING PATTERN: All descriptions of blue, azure, sapphire, etc. objects

20,000 Leagues Under the Sea, Jules Verne
The Doomed Planet, L. Ron Hubbard
A Fringe of Leaves, Patrick White
The Heat Death of the Universe, Pamela Zoline
Mother Night, Kurt Vonnegut

IV. BEING THE AGONIZING ACCOUNT . . .

GUIDING PATTERN: Fictional descriptions of libraries, bookshelves, and books
PHASE OF HERO'S JOURNEY: "Meeting the Mentor"

1984, George Orwell
City of God, E. L. Doctorow
A Clockwork Orange, Anthony Burgess
Contact, Carl Sagan
Crime and Punishment, Fyodor Dostoevsky
The Da Vinci Code, Dan Brown
Dawn, Octavia Butler
Don Quixote, Miguel De Cervantes
Dune, Frank Herbert
Fahrenheit 451, Ray Bradbury
Finnegans Wake, James Joyce
The Hitchhiker's Guide to the Galaxy, Douglas Adams
Interview with the Vampire, Anne Rice
Jude the Obscure, Thomas Hardy
Parable of the Sower, Octavia Butler
The Patchwork Girl of Oz, L. Frank Baum

The Poisonwood Bible, Barbara Kingsolver
Radio Free Albemuth, Philip K. Dick
The Return of the King, J. R. R. Tolkien
The Road, Cormac McCarthy
A Time to Kill, John Grisham

V. BEING THE CONTENTS OF THE BOOK

GUIDING PATTERN: MacGuffin collage 1. Descriptions of MacGuffins, other narrative-driving objects, and their backstories
PHASE OF HERO'S JOURNEY: "Meeting the Mentor"

Centennial, James Michener
Chains of Command, Marko Kloos
The High Window, Raymond Chandler
The Hunters of Dune, Brian Herbert and Kevin J. Anderson
The Lost World, Michael Crichton
The Maltese Falcon, Dashiell Hammett
Pawn of Prophecy, David Eddings
The Regulators, Richard Bachman
Time Out of Joint, Philip K. Dick

VI. BEING A VISUAL REPRESENTATION . . .

GUIDING PATTERN: Illustrations and other visual elements from novels
PHASE OF HERO'S JOURNEY: "Meeting the Mentor"

The Age of Innocence, Edith Wharton
At Swim-Two-Birds, Flann O'Brien
Blood and Guts in High School, Kathy Acker
Flaubert's Parrot, Julian Barnes
How to Be Both, Ali Smith
Infinite Jest, David Foster Wallace
Jealousy, Alain Robbe Grillet
Life: A User's Manual, Georges Perec
The Life and Opinions of Tristram Shandy, Gentleman, Laurence Sterne
Moby-Dick, Herman Melville
Mumbo Jumbo, Ishmael Reed
The Pickwick Papers, Charles Dickens
Rabbit Redux, John Updike
The Savage Detectives, Roberto Bolaño
Slaughterhouse-Five, Kurt Vonnegut
Watt, Samuel Beckett

VII. BEING THE EVENTS OF THE FOLLOWING . . .

GUIDING PATTERN: Descriptions of running and jogging
PHASE OF HERO'S JOURNEY: "Crossing the Threshold"

The Adventures of Huckleberry Finn, Mark Twain
The Adventures of Sherlock Holmes, Arthur Conan Doyle

The Art of Fielding, Chad Harbach
The Bourne Identity, Robert Ludlum
The Castle of Otranto, Horace Walpole
Church, Joseph W. Michels
Clarissa, Samuel Richardson
Crash, J. G. Ballard
Cropper's Cabin, Jim Thompson
The Da Vinci Code, Dan Brown
Dawn, Octavia Butler
Dhalgren, Samuel R. Delany
The Dispossesed, Ursula K. Le Guin
Do Androids Dream of Electric Sheep?, Philip K. Dick
Execution Dock, Anne Perry
A Farewell to Arms, Ernest Hemingway
Forrest Gump, Winston Groom
Frankenstein, Mary Shelley
A Game of Thrones, George R. R. Martin
The Great American Novel, Philip Roth
Harry Potter and the Sorcerer's Stone, J. K. Rowling
Ice, Anna Kavan
Interview with the Vampire, Anne Rice
The Italian, Ann Radcliffe
Jurassic Park, Michael Crichton
Koko, Peter Straub
Logan's Run, William F. Nolan
Lord of the Flies, William Golding
Marathon Man, William Goldman
A Maze of Death, Philip K. Dick
Murder in Retrospect, Agatha Christie
The Murder of Roger Ackroyd, Agatha Christie
The Murder on the Links, Agatha Christie
Neuromancer, William Gibson
Northanger Abbey, Jane Austen
The Notebook, Nicholas Sparks
Nova, Samuel R. Delany
The Old Curiosity Shop, Charles Dickens
Oliver Twist, Charles Dickens
Once a Runner, John L. Parker Jr.
The Pickwick Papers, Charles Dickens
The Princess Bride, William Goldman
Proof, Dick Francis
The Protector, David Morrell
Rabbit, Run, John Updike
Reamde, Neal Stephenson
The Return of the King, J. R. R. Tolkien
Rogue Male, Geoffrey Household
The Runner, Cynthia Voight
Running Dog, Don DeLillo
The Running Man, Richard Bachman
A Scanner Darkly, Philip K. Dick
The Other, David Guterson
Underworld, Don DeLillo
A Walk to Remember, Nicholas Sparks
We Have Always Lived in the Castle, Shirley Jackson
A Wild Sheep Chase, Haruki Murakami
Zone One, Colson Whitehead

VIII. BEING AN ACCOUNT OF THE SOMETHING . . .

GUIDING PATTERN: Moments of something being "out there," mostly from horror novels

PHASE OF HERO'S JOURNEY: "The Special World"

The Beasts in the Void, Paul W. Fairman
Bloodwinter, Tom Deitz
Bright Light City, Michael Hodjera
The Cabin in the Woods: The Official Movie Novelization, Tim Lebbon
Copper Coleson's Ghost, Edward P. Hendrick
Deadman Switch, Timothy Zahn
The Demigods of Olympus, Rick Riordan
Expedition, Gerald Breckenridge
Generation Warriors, Anne McCaffrey
Happy Days for Boys and Girls, Various Authors
The Heritage of the Desert, Zane Grey
Hideaway, Dean R. Koontz
In the Dark of the Night, John Saul
Isobel, James Oliver Curwood
Kenobi's Blade, Rebecca Moesta
The Legacy of Heorot, Larry Niven, Jerry Pournelle, and Steven Barnes
Less Than Zero, Bret Easton Ellis
Monster, Frank E. Peretti
The Radio Boys Rescue the Lost Alaska Expedition, Gerald Breckenridge
Revenant, Mel Odom
The Road, Cormac McCarthy
Rough Beast, Roger Dee
Sanctuary for a Lady, Naomi Rawlings
Sleeping Fires, Gertrude Atherton
Tom Fairfield in Camp, Allen Chapman
Winter Moon, Dean Koontz
Zombies Sold Separately, Cheyenne McCray

IX. BEING THE SIBILANT SOUNDS . . .

GUIDING PATTERN: Monster sounds from vintage comic books
PHASE OF HERO'S JOURNEY: "The Special World"

"HRROOGA! And Other Vintage Comic Book Monster Sounds," Yeoman Lowbrow for Flashbak.com

X. BEING THE TWO ROUTES BEFORE ME . . .

GUIDING PATTERN: Story options from choose your own adventure books
PHASE OF HERO'S JOURNEY: "The Special World"

The Cave of Time, Edward Packard
The Deadly Shadow, Richard Brightfield
The Forbidden Castle, Edward Packard
The Mystery of Chimney Rock, Edward Packard
Return to the Cave of Time, Edward Packard

XI. BEING THE CONTINUATION OF COLUMN B

GUIDING PATTERN: B sounds from books that begin with "B" (for and after Jez Burrows)

PHASE OF HERO'S JOURNEY: "The Special World"

Adventures of Bindle, Herbert George Jenkins
Babbitt, Sinclair Lewis
Babel-17, Samuel R. Delany
The Bad Beginning, Lemony Snicket
Bag of Bones, Stephen King
The Barrier, Rex Beach
Beric the Briton, G. A. Henty
Black Beauty, Anna Sewell
Brethren, John Grisham
The House on the Borderland, William Hope Hodgson

XII. BEING THE CONTINUATION OF THE CONT ...

GUIDING PATTERN: MacGuffin collage 2. False MacGuffins and power struggles regarding MacGuffins

PHASE OF HERO'S JOURNEY: "The Special World"

The Bacillus of Beauty, Harriet Stark
The Case-Book of Sherlock Holmes, Arthur Conan Doyle
The High Window, Raymond Chandler
In the Name of a Woman, Arthur W. Marchmont
The Indiscretion of the Duchess, Anthony Hope
The Maltese Falcon, Dashiell Hammett
The Night of the Trolls, Keith Laumer
On Board the Esmeralda, John Conroy Hutcheson

XIII. BEING THE CONTINUATION OF THE CONT ...

GUIDING PATTERN: More story options from choose your own adventure books

PHASE OF HERO'S JOURNEY: "The Special World"

The Cave of Time, Edward Packard
The Deadly Shadow, Richard Brightfield
The Mystery of Chimney Rock, Edward Packard
Return to the Cave of Time, Edward Packard

XIV. BEING THE ACCURATE ACCOUNT ...

GUIDING PATTERN: Time markers from all kinds of novels (after Christian Marclay)

PHASE OF HERO'S JOURNEY: "The Special World"

1984, George Orwell
The Adventures of Huckleberry Finn, Mark Twain
The Adventures of Sherlock Holmes, Arthur Conan Doyle
The Adventures of Tom Sawyer, Mark Twain
Black Beauty, Anna Sewell
The Bourne Identity, Robert Ludlum
The Catcher in the Rye, J. D. Salinger
Complete Story of the San Francisco Horror, Richard Linthicum, Trumbull White, and Samuel Fallows
The Conquest, Oscar Micheaux
Crooked House, Agatha Christie
The Da Vinci Code, Dan Brown
Disturbia, Christopher Fowler
Dracula, Bram Stoker
The Drowned World, J. G. Ballard
Finnegans Wake, James Joyce
The First Men in the Moon, Jules Verne
For Jacinta, Harold Bindloss
Gravity's Rainbow, Thomas Pynchon
Great Expectations, Charles Dickens
Go Tell It on the Mountain, James Baldwin
The House on the Borderland, William Hope Hodgson
Hunted and Harried, R. M. Ballantyne
The Idiot, Fyodor Dostoevsky
Jane Eyre, Charlotte Brontë
Light in August, William Faulkner
The Lion, the Witch and the Wardrobe, C. S. Lewis
Little Women, Louisa May Alcott
Molloy, Samuel Beckett
Murder on the Orient Express, Agatha Christie
The Nest of the Sparrowhawk, Baroness Orczy
Night and Day, Virginia Woolf
The Old Curiosity Shop, Charles Dickens
On the Beach, Neville Shute
On the Road, Jack Kerouac
O Pioneers!, Willa Cather
Persuasion, Jane Austen
The Phantom of the Opera, Gaston Leroux
The Picture of Dorian Gray, Oscar Wilde
The Pilgrim's Progress, John Bunyan
A Poor Man's House, Stephen Reynolds
The Shining, Stephen King
Swann's Way, Marcel Proust
The Turn of the Screw, Henry James
A Wild Sheep Chase, Haruki Murakami
Wuthering Heights, Emily Brontë

XV. BEING THE BALLAD OF . . .

GUIDING PATTERN: Poetry in novels
PHASE OF HERO'S JOURNEY: "The Special World"

Gravity's Rainbow, Thomas Pynchon
McTeague, Frank Norris

Pale Fire, Vladimir Nabokov
Pamela, Samuel Richardson
The Pickwick Papers, Charles Dickens
The Sot-Weed Factor, John Barth
Venus in Furs, Leopold von Sacher-Masoch
War and Peace, Leo Tolstoy
Waverley, Sir Walter Scott

XVI. BEING MY BRIEF ASCENT . . .

GUIDING PATTERN: Castle descriptions
PHASE OF HERO'S JOURNEY: "The Special World"

The Claiming of Sleeping Beauty, Anne Rice
Dracula, Bram Stoker
A Game of Thrones, George R. R. Martin
Great Expectations, Charles Dickens
Harry Potter and the Philosopher's Stone, J. K. Rowling
The Monk, M. G. Lewis
The Mysteries of Udolpho, Ann Radcliffe
The Return of the King, J .R. R. Tolkien
A Tale of Two Cities, Charles Dickens
Titus Groan, Mervyn Peake

XVII. BEING THE PAINTINGS THAT LINED . . .

GUIDING PATTERN: Visual descriptions of monsters from premodern fiction
PHASE OF HERO'S JOURNEY: "Approaching the Innermost Cave"

Carmilla, Sheridan Le Fanu
Dracula, Bram Stoker
Dr. Jekyll and Mr. Hyde, Robert Louis Stevenson
Frankenstein, Mary Shelley
The Great God Pan, Arthur Machen
The Man of the Crowd, Edgar Allan Poe
The Sandman, E. T. A. Hoffman

XVIII. BEING MY DECOROUS DESCENT . . .

GUIDING PATTERN: Descriptions of red and black objects and settings from Gothic fiction, red and black being the most common colors in this genre
PHASE OF HERO'S JOURNEY: "Approaching the Innermost Cave"

Carmilla, Sheridan Le Fanu
The Castle of Otranto, Horace Wapole
Collected Stories, Edgar Allan Poe
Collected Stories, Guy de Maupassant
Collected Stories, Nathaniel Hawthorne
The Confessions of an English Opium-Eater, Thomas De Quincey
Dr. Jekyll and Mr. Hyde, Robert Louis Stevenson
Dracula, Bram Stoker

Frankenstein, Mary Shelley
The History of the Caliph Vathek, William Beckford
Jane Slayre, Sherri Browning Erwin
Lock and Key Library, Julian Hawthorne, Ed.
The Monk, M. G. Lewis
The Monkey's Paw, W. W. Jacobs
The Mysteries of Udolpho, Ann Radcliffe
Nightmare Abbey, Thomas Love Peacock
Northanger Abbey, Jane Austen
The Phantom of the Opera, Gaston Leroux
The Picture of Dorian Gray, Oscar Wilde
The Private Memoirs and Confessions of a Justified Sinner, James Hogg
The Sword of the Lictor, Gene Wolfe
Things as They Are, William Godwin
The Turn of the Screw, Henry James
The Vampyre, John William Polidori
Wieland, Charles Brockden Brown
Wuthering Heights, Emily Brontë
The Yellow Wallpaper, Charlotte Perkins Gilman

XIX. BEING THE CLIMAX OF THIS NOVEL

GUIDING PATTERN: Exclamations and sudden utterances from pre-modern novels

PHASE OF HERO'S JOURNEY: "Approaching the Innermost Cave"

The Adventures of Dick Trevanion, Herbert Strang
The Adventures of Sherlock Holmes, Sir Arthur Conan Doyle
Anne of Green Gables, Lucy Maud Montgomery
Bernard Brooks' Adventures, Horatio Alger Jr.
The Cardinal's Snuff box, Henry Harland
Carolyn of the Corners, Ruth Belmore Endicott
A Christian Woman, Emilia Pardo Bazán
The Duke's Children, Anthony Trollope
Esther, Rosa Nouchette Carey
From Farm to Fortune, Horatio Alger Jr.
The Frontiersman, H. A. Cody
Gala-Days, Gail Hamilton
Grace Harlowe's First Year at Overton College, Jessie Graham Flower
Grisly Grisell, Charlotte M. Yonge
Guy Mannering, Sir Walter Scott
Hilda Lessways, Arnold Bennett
The Hunchback of Notre-Dame, Victor Hugo
In the Closed Room, Frances Hodgson Burnett
I Walked in Arden, Jack Crawford
The Ivory Snuff Box, Arnold Fredericks
The Land of Joy, Ralph Henry Barbour
The Laughing Cavalier, Baroness Orczy
The Little Grey House, Marion Ames Taggart
The Little Warrior, P. G. Wodehouse
Missy, Dana Gatlin

Mother, Maksim Gorky
My Ántonia, Willa Cather
Off on a Comet or Hector Servadac, Jules Verne
The Re-Creation of Brian Kent, Harold Bell Wright
The Red Badge of Courage, Stephen Crane
Riders of the Purple Sage, Zane Grey
Ten Thousand a-Year, Samuel Warren
When the World Shook, H. Rider Haggard
Woven with the Ship, Cyrus Townsend Brady

XX. BEING THE TATTERED TESTIMONY . . .

GUIDING PATTERN: Intentionally obscured proper nouns and profanities, along with other excessive uses of punctuation, from mostly pre-modern novels
PHASE OF HERO'S JOURNEY: "Approaching the Innermost Cave"

Anna Karenina, Leo Tolstoy
Bleak House, Charles Dickens
Catch-22, Joseph Heller
Crime and Punishment, Fyodor Dostoevsky
Dracula, Bram Stoker
Emma, Jane Austen
Fanny Hill, John Cleland
The Hermit of ——— Street, Anna Katharine Green
The Fortunes and Misfortunes of the Famous Moll Flanders, Daniel Defoe
Foucault's Pendulum, Umberto Eco
Frankenstein, Mary Shelley
Hopalong Cassidy's Rustler Round-Up, Clarence Edward Mulford
The Idiot, Fyodor Dostoevsky
Jane Eyre, Charlotte Brontë
Lady Susan, Jane Austen
L'Assommoir, Emile Zola
The Last Man, Mary Shelley
The Laughing Cavallier, Baroness Orczy
Les Misérables, Victor Hugo
The Life and Opinions of Tristram Shandy, Gentleman, Laurence Sterne
Lord Tony's Wife, Baroness Orczy
Mansfield Park, Jane Austen
Moby-Dick, Herman Melville
Northanger Abbey, Jane Austen
Pelham, Edward Bulwer Lytton
The Pickwick Papers, Charles Dickens
The Professor, Charlotte Brontë
Rob Roy, Sir Walter Scott
Sense and Sensibility, Jane Austen
Sketches by Seymour, Robert Seymour
A Study in Scarlet, Arthur Conan Doyle
The Time Machine, H. G. Wells
Treasure Island, Robert Louis Stevenson
Under Western Eyes, Joseph Conrad
The Vampyre, John William Polidori
War and Peace, Leo Tolstoy
The Wonderful Adventures of Nils, Selma Lagerlöf

XXI. BEING MY FATEFUL FIGHT . . .

GUIDING PATTERN: MacGuffin collage 3. Moments of the MacGuffins being lost, etc.

PHASE OF HERO'S JOURNEY: "The Ordeal"

Artist and Model, René de Pont-Jest
Asneha: The Legend of the Opal, Carlo De Fornaro
Aunt Fanny's Story-Book for Little Boys and Girls, Frances Elizabeth Barrow
Beyond the Rocks, Elinor Glyn
Catherine, William Makepeace Thackeray
The Chamber of Life, Green Peyton Wertenbaker
The Code of the Woosters, P. G. Wodehouse
Contraband, E. R. Spencer
Egholm and His God, Johannes Buchholtz
The Eyes of the World, Harold Bell Wright
Fairy-Book, Edmund Dulac
The Flight of the Shadow, George MacDonald
Glory Road, Robert A. Heinlein
The Gloved Hand, Burton E. Stevenson
Grace Harlowe's Sophomore Year at High School, Jessie Graham Flower
The Hickory Limb, Parker Fillmore
The High Window, Raymond Chandler
Highland Ballad, Christopher Leadem
His Hour, Elinor Glyn
The Intrusion of Jimmy, P. G. Wodehouse
Irresolute Catherine, Violet Jacob
I Walked in Arden, Jack Crawford
The Link, Alan Edward Nourse
Lord Lundy's Snuff Box, William Mackay
The Maltese Falcon, Dashiell Hammett
The Man Who Drove the Car, Max Pemberton
Martian Nightmare, Bryce Walton
Michael, E. F. Benson
The Minister's Wife, Margaret Oliphant
Monster of the Asteroid, Ray Cummings
My Beautiful Lady, Thomas Woolner
My Book of Favourite Fairy Tales, Edric Vredenburg
A Noble Name, Claire Von Glümer
The Pearl of Love, Madeline Leslie
Port Argent, Arthur Colton
Project Mastodon, Clifford Donald Simak
Rachel Ray, Anthony Trollope
Raftmates, Kirk Munroe
Redburn, Herman Melville
The Risk Profession, Donald E. Westlake
Sheaves, E. F. Benson
The Story of a Pioneer, Anna Howard Shaw
Sudden Jim, Clarence Budington Kelland
The Sundial, Fred M. White
Things as They Are, William Godwin
The Three Imposters, Arthur Machen

Traitor and True, John Bloundelle-Burton
Where the Red Fern Grows, Wilson Rawls
Withered Leaves, Rudolf von Gottschall

XXII. BEING THE TYPO-TORTURED TALE . . .

GUIDING PATTERN: Typos from first editions of novels
PHASE OF HERO'S JOURNEY: "The Reward"

The Adventures of Huckleberry Finn, Mark Twain
Against the Day, Thomas Pynchon
All the King's Men, Robert Penn Warren
The Amazing Adventures of Kavalier & Clay, Michael Chabon
An American Tragedy, Theodore Dreiser
American Pastoral, Philip Roth
Angle of Repose, Wallace Stegner
Anna Karenina, Leo Tolstoy
Anthony Adverse, Hervey Allen
The Captive & The Fugitive, Marcel Proust
Cat's Cradle, Kurt Vonnegut
Chesapeake, James A. Michener
Cloud Atlas, David Mitchell
The Count of Monte Cristo, Alexandre Dumas
The Crossing, Cormac McCarthy
Cryptonomicon, Neal Stephenson
Dark Eagle, John Ensor Harr
Don Quixote, Miguel De Cervantes
The Echo Maker, Richard Powers
The Elegance of the Hedgehog, Muriel Barbery
Erik Dorn, Ben Hecht
Everville, Clive Barker
Foucault's Pendulum, Umberto Eco
Foundation, Isaac Asimov
Foundation and Empire, Isaac Asimov
The Gardener's Son, Cormac McCarthy
Ghostwalk, Rebecca Stott
Grave Goods, Ciara Graves
Gravity's Rainbow, Thomas Pynchon
The Heart Is a Lonely Hunter, Carson McCullers
Historic Oddities and Strange Events, Sabine Baring-Gould
The Hystery of the Broken Fether, Allison Muri
Infinite Jest, David Foster Wallace
It, Stephen King
Ivanhoe, Sir Walter Scott
A Jay of Italy, Bernard Capes
Jo's Boys, Louisa May Alcott
King Silky!, Leo Rosten
Kings of the Earth, Jon Clinch
Libra, Don DeLillo
The Lost Wagon, James Arthur Kjelgaard
A Man in Full, Tom Wolfe
Moonfall, Jack McDevitt
The Nature Book, Tom Comitta
Of Time and the River, Thomas Wolfe
The Old Man in the Corner, Baroness Orczy
Peter Pan and Wendy, J. M. Barrie
Piano Stories, Felisberto Hernandez

The Pillars of the Earth, Ken Follett
The Poet at the Breakfast-Table, Oliver Wendell Holmes
A Portrait of the Artist as a Young Man, James Joyce
The Queen's Governess, Karen Harper
Shining City, Seth Greenland
Sonya Babushka, Maurice Chideckel
A Stay Against Confusion, Ron Hansen
The Story of Edgar Sawtelle, David Wroblewski
The Strange Story of Rab Ráby, Mór Jókai
Summerland, Michael Chabon
Tropic of Cancer, Henry Miller
Under the Volcano, Malcolm Lowry
What I Lived For, Joyce Carol Oates
Within a Budding Grove, Marcel Proust
Zero History, William Gibson

XXIII. BEING THE SHORT SHORT STORY . . .

GUIDING PATTERN: Instances of "the sun had not yet risen," the first line from Virginia Woolf's *The Waves*, as found in multiple novels
PHASE OF HERO'S JOURNEY: "The Reward"

The Bible in Spain, George Borrow
Budd Boyd's Triumph, William Pendleton Chipman
The Burden, Stephen Lucas
Case with 4 Clowns: A Sergeant Beef Mystery, Leo Bruce
The Childhood of King Erik Menved, Bernhard Severin Ingemann
The Cid Campeador, Antonio de Trueba
From Siberia to Switzerland, William Westall
Grampa in Oz, Ruth Plumly Thompson
Green Mansions, William Henry Hudson
Lincoln, Gore Vidal
Messenger No. 48, James Otis
The Old Chelsea Bun-House, Anne Manning
The Orange Fairy Book, Andrew Lang, Ed.
Quinneys, Horace Annesley Vachell
Return from the Stars, Stanislaw Lem
The Rushton Boys at Treasure Cove, Spencer Davenport
Squire Arden, Margaret Oliphant
The Thorn in the Nest, Martha Finley
Top of the World Stories for Boys and Girls, Emilie Poulsson and Laura E. Poulsson
The Trail of the Elk, Mikkjel Fonhus
Under St. Paul's, Richard Dowling
The Wagnerian Romances, Gertrude Hall

XXIV. BEING A VISUAL RENDERING . . .

GUIDING PATTERN: Illustrations from Charles Dickens novels
PHASE OF HERO'S JOURNEY: "The Road Back"

XXV. BEING AN OLFACTORY RENDERING . . .

GUIDING PATTERN: Olfactory descriptions
PHASE OF HERO'S JOURNEY: "The Road Back"

Absalom, Absalom!, William Faulkner
The Awakening, Kate Chopin
Clockers, Richard Price
Cold Black Hearts, Jeffrey J. Mariotte
The Corner House Girls in a Play, Grace Brooks Hill
Dorothy Harcourt's Secret, Emma Southworth
The First Men in the Moon, H. G. Wells
From the Life of a Good-for-Nothing, Joseph von Eichendorff
Hobee's Quest, Robert B. Chambers
L'Assommoir, Emile Zola
Light in August, William Faulkner
Love in the Time of Cholera, Gabriel García Márquez
Perfume, Patrick Suskind
Pinocchio, Carlo Collodi
A Siren, Thomas Adolphus Trollope
Swann's Way, Marcel Proust
Vandover and the Brute, Frank Norris

XXVI. BEING THE DISCREET DREAMS . . .

GUIDING PATTERN: Moments of "and then I woke up" and the like
PHASE OF HERO'S JOURNEY: "The Road Back"

The Ax, Donald E. Westlake
Be Here to Love Me at the End of the World, Sasha Fletcher
The Black Bag, Louis Joseph Vance
The Book of Gud, Dan Spain and Harold Hersey
The Catcher in the Rye, J. D. Salinger
A Clockwork Orange, Anthony Burgess
The Crystal Ball, Roy J. Snell
A Daughter of the Morning, Zona Gale
Dracula, Bram Stoker
The Dream, H. G. Wells
The Easiest Way, Eugene Walter and Arthur Hornblow
The Fever, Wallace Shawn
The High Window, Raymond Chandler
Journey to the End of the Night, Louis-Ferdinand Céline
Junky, William S. Burroughs
Kafka on the Shore, Haruki Murakami
King of Shadows, Susan Cooper
The Lathe of Heaven, Ursula K. Le Guin
Memnoch the Devil, Ann Rice
The Night Operator, Frank L. Packard
The Nose, Nikolai Gogol
Obsidian Fate, Diana G. Gallagher
The Sandman, E. T. A. Hoffman
Sometimes a Great Notion, Ken Kesey
The Stranger, Albert Camus
The Virgin of Valkarion, Poul Anderson
Vertigo, Bob Shaw

A Wild Sheep Chase, Haruki Murakami
Wings Over the Rockies, Ambrose Newcomb

XXVII. BEING THE AWKWARD ACCOUNT . . .

GUIDING PATTERN: Mostly pre-duel language—the instigation of the duel to the anticipation the night before—from fiction about dueling or predominantly featuring a duel

PHASE OF HERO'S JOURNEY: "The Resurrection"

The Diary of a Superfluous Man, Ivan Turgenev
The Duel, Anton Chekhov
The Duel, Joseph Conrad
The Duel, O. Henry
The Duel, Heinrich von Kleist
The Duel, Alexander Kuprin
Gulliver's Travels, Jonathan Swift
Jane Eyre, Charlotte Brontë
Wonder Tales from Tibet, Eleanore Myers Jewett

FOOTNOTE GUIDING PATTERN: All beard descriptions from *White-Jacket* by Herman Melville

XXVIII. BEING THE DAY OF THE DUEL

GUIDING PATTERN: More pre-duel language—the day of and everything up to the shot

PHASE OF HERO'S JOURNEY: "The Resurrection"

The Boy Scouts of the Eagle Patrol, Howard Payson
The Diary of a Superfluous Man, Ivan Turgenev
The Duel, Anton Chekhov
The Duel, Joseph Conrad
The Duel, O. Henry
The Duel, Heinrich von Kleist
The Duel, Alexander Kuprin

XXIX. BEING THE SOUNDS THE BIRDS MADE . . .

GUIDING PATTERN: Bird sounds from novels

PHASE OF HERO'S JOURNEY: "The Resurrection"

Big Sur, Jack Kerouac
Jonathan Livingston Seagull, Richard Bach
Lady Chatterley's Lover, D. H. Lawrence
Little House on the Prairie, Laura Ingalls Wilder

Moby-Dick, Herman Melville
Sometimes a Great Notion, Ken Kesey
Sons and Lovers, D. H. Lawrence
A Tale for the Time Being, Ruth Ozeki
Tess of the D'Urbervilles, Thomas Hardy
Ulysses, James Joyce
The White Peacock, D. H. Lawrence

XXX. BEING THE RIVETING RESULTS . . .

GUIDING PATTERN: More dueling language—the moments following the shot
PHASE OF HERO'S JOURNEY: "The Resurrection"

The Diary of a Superfluous Man, Ivan Turgenev
The Duel, Anton Chekhov
The Duel, Joseph Conrad
The Duel, O. Henry
The Duel, Alexander Kuprin
The Duel, Heinrich von Kleist

XXXI. BEING THE GOLDEN PRELUDE . . .

GUIDING PATTERN: Yellow, gold, amber, etc. descriptions
PHASE OF HERO'S JOURNEY: "Return with the Elixir"

£19,000, Burford Delannoy
Beyond the Vanishing Point, Raymond King Cummings
The Bird in the Box, Mary Mears
Brother and Sister, Josephine Lawrence
The Collected Works of Ambrose Bierce, Ambrose Bierce
The Colonel of the Red Huzzars, John Reed Scott
Crome Yellow, Aldous Huxley
The Drums of War, Henry De Vere Stacpoole
Four Arthurian Romances, Chrétien DeTroye
Four Meetings, Henry James
The Garden of the Plynck, Karle Wilson Baker
Golden Dicky, Marshall Saunders
The Golden Woman, Ridgwell Cullum
How the Fairy Violet Lost and Won Her Wings, Marianne L. B. Ker
Marie, H. Rider Haggard
Mountain, Clement Wood
The Mysteries of Udolpho, Anne Radcliffe
The Outdoor Girls at Ocean View, Laura Lee Hope
Pickle the Spy, Andrew Lang
The Promised Land, Mary Antin
The Sky Trap, Frank Belknap Long
The Star-Gazers, George Manville Fenn
Stopover Planet, Robert E. Gilbert
The Story of Charles Strange, Mrs. Henry Wood
Swann's Way, Marcel Proust
Wilt Thou Torchy, Sewell Ford
The Wizard of Oz, L. Frank Baum

XXXII. BEING THE END OF THIS NOVEL . . .

GUIDING PATTERN: Last lines from novels and one short story
PHASE OF HERO'S JOURNEY: "The Ordinary World Returns"

After London, Richard Jefferies
Armageddon—2419 A.D., Philip Francis Nowlan
Atonement, Ian McEwan
Before I Die, Jenny Downham
Brave New World, Aldous Huxley
Breaking Dawn, Stephenie Meyer
A Christmas Carol, Charles Dickens
A Clockwork Orange, Anthony Burgess
Devil in a Blue Dress, Walter Mosley
Finnegans Wake, James Joyce
For Whom the Bell Tolls, Ernest Hemingway
Gilead, Marilynne Robinson
The Grapes of Wrath, John Steinbeck
Great Expectations, Charles Dickens
Harry Potter and the Deathly Hallows, J. K. Rowling
The House of the Wolf, Stanley J. Weyman
The Land That Time Forgot, Edgar Rice Burroughs
The Lost Stradivarius, J. Meade Falkner
Man and Wife, Tony Parsons
The Mantooth, Christopher Leadem
The Marriage Plot, Jeffrey Eugenides
Memoirs of a Geisha, Arthur Golden
The Metamorphosis, Franz Kafka
Molloy, Samuel Beckett
Mrs. Dalloway, Virginia Woolf
Out, Ronald Sukenick
Andy Grant's Pluck, Andy Grant
Reached, Ally Condie
Rebecca, Daphne du Maurier
The Red Thumb Mark, R. Austin Freeman
Sarah's Key, Tatiana de Rosnay
The Sheltering Sky, Paul Bowles
The Tree of Man, Patrick White
Ubik, Philip K. Dick
Underworld, Don DeLillo
Watership Down, Richard Adams
What We Talk About When We Talk About Love, Raymond Carver
Wild Swans, Jung Chang

ACKNOWLEDGEMENTS

This book is dedicated to my editor Lizzie Davis in celebration of her work at Coffee House Press and beyond. I owe so much to Lizzie's belief in my work and am grateful to count her as a friend.

A mountain of thanks is due to the larger Coffee House team that made *Patchwork* possible throughout its publishing journey: Kristen Bledsoe, Anitra Budd, Jeremy Davies, Daphne DiFazio, Robyn Earhart, Linda Ewing, Clara Geze, Laura Graveline, Mark Haber, Rachel Holscher, Melanie Kleiss, Ülrika Moats, Abbie Phelps, Erika Stephens, and Quynh Van. Thank you for making Coffee House not only a publishing house but a true community. And a big thank you is also due to Sarah Evenson for the beautiful silk screen cover illustration.

I am so grateful to my agent Mariah Stovall for believing in this book and for guiding me along the way. And many thanks to the editors and organizations that published early excerpts from this book: Kelly Luce of *Electric Literature*; Sophia Wang and Lisa Rybovich Crallé of Heavy Breathing; Paul Yoon and Laura van den Berg, guest editors of *The Kenyon Review*.

Unending thanks and love to Medaya Ocher and Simone Rose for their daily support and inspiration. And to my family and friends who've stuck with me through it all.

Coffee House Press began as a small letterpress operation in 1972 and has grown into an internationally renowned nonprofit publisher of literary fiction, essay, poetry, and other work that doesn't fit neatly into genre categories.

LITERATURE
is not the same thing as
PUBLISHING

FUNDER ACKNOWLEDGMENTS

Coffee House Press is an internationally renowned independent book publisher and arts nonprofit based in Minneapolis, MN; through its literary publications, Coffee House acts as a catalyst and connector—between authors and readers, ideas and resources, creativity and community, inspiration and action.

Coffee House Press books are made possible through the generous support of grants and donations from corporations, state and federal grant programs, family foundations, and the many individuals who believe in the transformational power of literature. This activity is made possible by the voters of Minnesota through a Minnesota State Arts Board Operating Support grant, thanks to the legislative appropriation from the Arts and Cultural Heritage Fund. Coffee House also receives major operating support from the Amazon Literary Partnership, Jerome Foundation, Literary Arts Emergency Fund, McKnight Foundation, and the National Endowment for the Arts (NEA). To find out more about how NEA grants impact individuals and communities, visit www.arts.gov.

Coffee House Press receives additional support from Bookmobile; Dorsey & Whitney LLP; and the Schwab Charitable Fund.

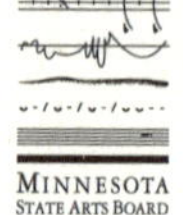

McKNIGHT FOUNDATION

THE PUBLISHER'S CIRCLE OF COFFEE HOUSE PRESS

Publisher's Circle members make significant contributions to Coffee House Press's annual giving campaign. Understanding that a strong financial base is necessary for the press to meet the challenges and opportunities that arise each year, this group plays a crucial part in the success of Coffee House's mission.

Recent Publisher's Circle members include many anonymous donors, Patricia A. Beithon, Robin Chemers Neustein, Kelli Cloutier, Theodore Cornwell, Jane Dalrymple-Hollo, Jeremy M. Davies, Mary Ebert and Paul Stembler, Kamilah Foreman, Eva Galiber, Roger Hale and Nor Hall, William Hardacker, Randy Hartten and Ron Lotz, Carl and Heidi Horsch, Amy L. Hubbard and Geoffrey J. Kehoe Fund of the St. Paul & Minnesota Foundation, Hyde Family Charitable Fund, Kenneth & Susan Kahn, the Kenneth Koch Literary Estate, Cinda Kornblum, the Lenfestey Family Foundation, Carol and Aaron Mack, Gillian McCain, Mary and Malcolm McDermid, Daniel N. Smith III and Maureen Millea Smith, Vance Opperman, Mr. Pancks' Fund in memory of Graham Kimpton, Alan Polsky, Robin Preble, Ronald Restrepo and Candace S. Baggett, Elizabeth Schnieders, Steve Smith, Jeffrey Sugerman and Sarah Schultz, Paul Thissen, Allyson Tucker, Grant Wood, Margaret Wurtele, Aptara Inc., Dorsey and Whitney Foundation.

For more information about the Publisher's Circle and other ways to support Coffee House Press books, authors, and activities, please visit www.coffeehousepress.org/pages/donate or contact us at info@coffeehousepress.org.

Tom Comitta is the author of *The Nature Book* (Coffee House Press) and *People's Choice Literature: The Most Wanted Novel and The Most Unwanted Novel* (Columbia University Press). Their fiction and essays have appeared in *WIRED*, *Literary Hub*, *Electric Literature*, *Los Angeles Review of Books*, *The Believer*, and *BOMB*. Comitta works as a book designer and lives in Los Angeles with their partner and child.

Patchwork was based on a design by
Bookmobile Design & Digital Publisher Services.
Text is set in Adobe Caslon Pro.